"What are we looking for? A trapdoor?" Scott asked.

"No." Abby chuckled, but it sounded strained. Then she lifted a rock, plucked a slender object from the earth and announced triumphantly, "This."

Abby wiped the key on her jeans and took the stairs two at a time. She slid the key into the deadbolt and opened the door to the keeper's quarters.

"I'm glad you came along today," Scott said.

"Thank me after we're rescued, okay?"

Scott spotted the radio communications box on the counter just as Abby reached it and began flipping switches, waiting impatiently and then scowling when she didn't get a response.

"I don't understand," she muttered, flipping a toggle up and down.

"I think I do." Scott reached past her to the lifeless power cord. He held up the severed end for her to see. "It's been cut."

RACHELLE MCCALLA

ate seventeen pounds of chocolate while writing this book. She also did 143 loads of laundry during that same time, and thinks folding towels is one of the best cures for writer's block (the other best cures are exercise and insomnia).

A graduate of Hastings College and the University of Dubuque Theological Seminary, Rachelle has lived in Iowa, Illinois, South Carolina (briefly!), and Wisconsin, and now makes Nebraska her home. When she's not writing, Rachelle spends most of her time at the church where her husband is pastor, or running after their four energetic children. For more information on forthcoming titles, plus fun background notes on the places and characters in this book, visit www.rachellemccalla.com. You can also find Rachelle on the message boards at www.eHarlequin.com.

Survival
INSTINCT

Rachelle
McCalla

Steeple
Hill®

Published by Steeple Hill Books™

STEEPLE HILL BOOKS

Steeple
Hill®

Recycling programs
for this product may
not exist in your area.

ISBN-13: 978-0-373-44383-3

SURVIVAL INSTINCT

Two are better than one because they have
a good return for their work:
if one falls down, his friend can help him up.
But pity the man who falls
and has no one to help him up!
—*Ecclesiastes* 4:9-10

To Ray, without whom there would be no book.

Acknowledgments

Thank you to the congregation of
Bayfield Presbyterian Church for calling us
to Bayfield. I would never have known there
was a Devil's Island if it hadn't been for you.

Thank you to everyone who takes the time to read
this book. I'm honored.

Thank you to Emily Rodmell, for believing my
manuscript could become a book.

And to Ms. Henre, for making me learn English.

And most importantly, to Jesus Christ, who brought
me to this place. Only You know what it cost to get
me here. Thank You.

PROLOGUE

Someone was watching her. Abby Caldwell clutched her keys and hastened her steps, reminding herself that for all the times she'd felt eyes on her over the past few weeks, she'd never actually seen anyone. For all she knew, the feeling was a figment of her imagination. Perhaps she was overworked and in need of a vacation.

Abby reached her back door and jammed the key in the lock. She'd half twisted the knob when a huge hand covered hers. A voice she thought she'd left behind years before rumbled above her ear. "Hey, Abby."

He must have seen she was about to scream, because his other hand immediately covered her mouth. "Don't get too excited. I just want to talk." He pulled his hand slowly away from her mouth.

Abby swallowed her cry and nodded, even though she didn't believe him. Trevor Price never just wanted to talk.

She tried to make her voice sound light, to play along. "I thought the Coast Guard had you stationed somewhere else. Near Canada?"

"I was." His voice sounded even more menacing than she remembered it. "I've been back for a few months now. I'm surprised you haven't seen me. I've seen plenty of you."

So she hadn't imagined the feeling of being watched. If the six-foot-five-inch gorilla hadn't been holding her wrist so tightly, she might have accused him of stalking her. Instead she asked in a whisper, "What do you want?"

"The ring."

Her heart beat so hard she thought she'd choke. "I don't have it," she told him honestly. She hadn't had it in years—not since she'd buried it, along with all its bitter memories, in the spot where he'd proposed to her on Devil's Island.

"Well, then, find it." Trevor trailed one finger down the side of her cheek, his icy eyes holding hers. "Or I'll have to come look for it myself."

Abby pinched her eyes shut. Trevor was a bully, that was all. And he couldn't bully her without her permission. She opened her eyes and stared him down.

"Why do you need it? Why now? It's been what—six years?"

His hand loosened slightly at her wrist. "Five. And that ring never should have been yours. I never should have proposed to you."

Finally, something they could both agree on. Their entire relationship had been the biggest mistake of her life, but she thought she'd put it behind her.

As she watched with fearful eyes wide, Trevor lifted Abby's left hand up in front of her face. He pinched her ring finger and slowly bent it back.

"It fit perfectly, didn't it?" Trevor's mouth hovered close to her ear. He pulled her finger back farther, and she blinked back tears. "Return the ring to me within forty-eight hours, or you won't have anywhere to wear it."

"But, I don't—" she started to protest.

"Find it!" He jerked her finger back until she thought it

would snap. "You have two days." With that, he dropped her hands, let her go and strode away.

Abby hurried to unlock her door and slid inside, locking it after her before Trevor could change his mind and come back. Then she leaned against the door frame and flexed her fingers, the lowest joint of her ring finger throbbing where Trevor had wrenched it.

She wasn't sure exactly what his threat meant, but she knew Trevor Price enough to know he wouldn't have any qualms about following through with it. If she didn't get the ring to him within two days, he'd cut off her finger—or worse.

ONE

The dark gray-blue water faded to the blue sky as the speedboat *Helene* cleared the western side of Bear Island and entered the open water of Lake Superior. Abby Caldwell shivered and pulled her jacket more snugly around her, glad she'd opted for the fleece-lined windbreaker instead of a sweater. October could be cold in northern Wisconsin, and it was invariably colder on the lake. She'd hoped this Saturday would turn out warm, but it was already midmorning and the sun had yet to peek out of the clouds.

Captain Sal steered the *Helene* east, at cross-angles with the waves that were higher here away from the protection of the islands. Abby felt the rhythmic slap, slap, slap as each wave smacked the twenty-foot craft, jarring her already nervous stomach. If she didn't fear Trevor Price so much, she would never be out on the deadly Gitche Gumee this late in the season.

She could see the autumn colors of Devil's Island in the distance, and though she'd never liked the island, she was glad to see it now. The sooner she got there, the sooner she'd be off the stomach-rocking boat and onto solid ground. And the sooner she'd be able to get the ring and Trevor out of her life for good.

Abby said a silent calming prayer and glanced over at the other passengers. She'd shared water taxi rides with tourists before, and was thankful to find this group less talkative than many. She wasn't in the mood to chat. To her relief, the three tourists were looking ahead to the island and appeared to have forgotten she was even with them. Abby squinted at the figure in the Northwoods College ball cap, the one closest to the boat's tiny cabin, the one with the broad shoulders and square set jaw.

She recognized him. It had been nine years since she'd last seen him, and though his face had grown firmer with age, the sight of him still set her insides quivering with awareness. Scott Frasier had been the star quarterback of the Northwoods College football team the year they'd almost won the championship, the only year they'd made it to the play-offs in college history. Everybody from Northwoods College knew Scott Frasier. According to the school's alumni magazine, he was a psychologist of some sort in the Twin Cities area now.

Scott wouldn't recognize her. She'd only been a freshman his senior year, and seniors never bothered with freshmen, even if they had been in the same poetry class fall semester, and often ended up in the same discussion group. In some ways, she was glad he wouldn't remember her, and equally grateful the noise of the boat and wind discouraged conversation. She didn't want to have to explain what she was doing on this trip.

The other two, a man and woman who looked to be in their early fifties, were probably Scott's parents. The woman looked like him, anyway, with the same statuesque height and aquiline nose. The man was certainly shorter, softer, rounder, but the way he clung on to the woman's side, he was bound to be her husband. Her fingers were covered with diamonds, and the particularly huge stone on the ring finger of her left hand matched the setting of the masculine ring he wore.

"Coming about," Captain Sal announced, his voice thick with a Wisconsin brogue. There had been a time when the accent would have sounded foreign to her ears, but after nearly a decade in northern Wisconsin, Abby would have probably pronounced it much the same way. She watched carefully as he steered the craft well wide of the southern tip of the island, knowing that even on the sandy side, boulders hid just below the surface, ready to scrape their underside and send the *Helene* sinking like the *Titanic*.

As soon as Sal had positioned the boat alongside the long wooden dock, Abby stood, ready to get on with her errand. Scott leaped agilely onto the faded wooden planks, then reached out toward her.

"Need a hand up?" he asked, his smile friendly.

Abby already had one hand on the high metal support that held the dock, and she'd never been one to lean on anybody. She gave a shrug and started to pull herself up, hoping he wouldn't think she was being rude. The idea of being in physical contact with him made her stomach flutter in a different sort of way than it had on the rough water of the lake.

Waves from the *Helene*'s wake hit the pier, rocking the boat in a dipping, unsteady rhythm. With one foot on the boat and one on the dock, Abby felt her legs wobbling madly beneath her, and she braced herself for the impact of the wooden planks as her face keeled toward them, while she clung to the metal support. The last thing she wanted was to end up in the cold water of Lake Superior.

Scott's arms were around her in an instant, hoisting her upward effortlessly. They stumbled backward together down the long dock for three or four steps before Abby managed to gain control of her feet. Her face pressed against the soft cotton of Scott's T-shirt where it was exposed by the open buttons of his quilted flannel shirt. For a moment, she was aware of the strong beat of his heart and the thick muscles that told her he hadn't lost his college football-player physique.

Then she pushed away, instantly self-conscious, as Sal's voice carried behind her. "Just wait till I get her tied up, now," he chided in his thick brogue.

"Are you all right?" Scott asked, peering into her face.

"Yes, fine." She brushed at her clothes as though she could as easily brush away the feeling of being in his arms. Oh, how the Abby of nine years ago would have swooned at the thought of that moment! "Thanks to you." She smiled up at him, trying to appear grateful and confident and not the least bit affected by him, though she was. Now she needed to get on with her hike and get away from him before she made an even bigger fool of herself.

She cleared her throat, which had gone inexplicably dry, and started off down the pier. The island drew her attention, so wild and remote, and so deceptively beautiful in its fall colors. Then she glanced back at the other couple, still on the boat, who appeared to be arguing in low tones. The woman grasped her necklace and shook her head firmly. Abby wanted to thank them for letting her share the water taxi out to the island, but at the same time, she didn't want to interrupt.

Turning her attention back to Scott, she smiled. "Thanks for the ride. I'm going to take a quick hike. I should be back here well within an hour."

"Take your time. We've hired Captain Sal for two hours. Where are you off to?"

"There's a lighthouse on the north side of the island," Abby explained simply, "and a road leading up there."

Scott looked off in the direction she'd indicated. "I might like to see that," he said in a musing voice, then looked back to the older couple. "But my mother will want to look for driftwood. I'll have to check it out later."

Impatient to get on with her search, Abby figured Scott's plans weren't any of her business. "Right. Thanks again." She threw a wave his way and headed up the dock, breathing deeply of the crisp air as the scent of the lake gave way to forest smells, pine and birch and hemlock, and the earthy aroma of wet fallen leaves. She had a mission to accomplish, and the chilling memory of Trevor's tight grip hastened her steps.

Abby tried to stick to the middle of the path, where a tangle of weeds gave the moist clay-topped drive some measure of traction. The rest of the road was slick from a heavy rain that had drenched the Apostle Islands and most of Lake Superior the night before, so Abby was glad for her thick-soled hiking boots. Still, keeping a fast pace was nearly impossible. When she spotted a sturdy-looking fallen tree branch, she snapped off the narrow end over her knee and used the remainder as a hiking stick, which gave her a greater measure of balance and allowed her to move more quickly.

In six minutes' time she'd reached the old keeper's quarters, where Coast Guardsmen had lodged year-round in the decades before the lighthouse had been automated. She'd been a tenant there, too, one summer. But that was a time she preferred not to think about.

The road leveled off and became a narrow, grass-matted path. Glad for the added traction, Abby dropped her walking stick and picked up her pace to a jog. Two minutes later, the woods opened up to the wide sea before her. Had the sky been clear, she could have seen the lake's northern shore, with Minnesota on the left and Canada off to the right. Instead an uncertain haze blanketed the horizon.

With a glance at the lighthouse to her right, Abby turned off the trail to her left, surprised at how quickly she was able to locate the narrow rabbit run she'd followed only twice before.

Her nervous stomach rose like a lump in her throat, and she realized she'd clenched her hands into tight fists. The ring finger on her left hand still ached, a reminder of Trevor's threat. Forcing herself to relax, she prayed silently, *Lord, please let the ring be there, and please help me find it.*

The small clearing hadn't changed, its brownstone outcropping as solid as the island itself. Abby spied the distinctly shaped rock quickly and dropped to her knees, praying again as she lifted it, her eyes blind to the brassy coiled centipedes and moss-gray roly-polies that fled for cover when she exposed them to the light.

The ring had not tarnished. Its gold was still vibrant, its central diamond brilliant. She grabbed it up, dropped the rock and poked the ring deep into the tiny fifth pocket of her jeans. Then she inhaled a cleansing breath and exhaled a prayer of thanks before heading back toward the dock.

The downhill trek seemed easier now, and though she slowed her pace, the hike of just over a mile passed quickly. As she reached the southern end of the island and stepped free of the woods, she saw Scott heading toward the dock with driftwood in his arms. He smiled as she approached. "Back so soon? That wasn't nearly an hour."

Abby shrugged. She didn't bother trying to fight back the smile she felt at seeing him. He was such a handsome man, and with the ring now safely in her pocket, she could relax a little and enjoy being on the island with him. "How's the search for driftwood going?"

Scott looked down at the meager pile of wood he'd set on the concrete slab at the head of the dock, then turned his head toward where the older couple walked along the rocky shore, nearly out of sight around the curve of the island. "My stepfather," he began, his eyes stormy, but then apparently decided against voicing his opinion. His expression softened. "I don't suppose you'd want to show me the lighthouse?"

His request brought a smile to Abby's lips in spite of the fear she still felt. He wanted to spend time with her, too? "I thought you were spending this trip with your mother."

"I have, and I will." His voice sounded resigned. "But I need a break. You were up there and back so quickly, and they're busy enough with their bickering I'm sure they'll hardly notice if I slip away." He looked imploringly toward her.

Abby's eyes widened and she looked him full in the face for the first time. From close-up his face appeared more manly than boyish, with smile creases branching out from his eyes. She realized how much they'd both aged since college. "Sure. It's right this way." Suddenly self-conscious, she diverted her eyes from his face and focused instead on watching her feet as they made their way up the slick path.

They reached the road and began the steady uphill trek.

The woods quickly closed in behind them. Abby felt she ought to make conversation with her hiking partner to break the awkward silence, but the only thing she could think of was the need to confess their shared history, however long ago it had been.

"You probably don't remember me," she started hesitantly, "but I believe we were at Northwoods College around the same time."

"Abby Caldwell," Scott stated with assurance. "We had a poetry class together."

Abby's heart nearly stopped, and one foot took a wild slip on a patch of slimy clay.

Scott grabbed her arm, steadying her. "I'm Scott Frasier, by the way." His grin was broad, and he looked pleased.

"I remember," she said breathlessly, far too aware of the stable, comforting grip of his hand on her arm. "You were on the football team. Starting quarterback. I went to every game."

Scott grinned. "So what are you up to these days?"

"I live and work in Bayfield." Abby tried to keep both her voice and feet steady as she continued up the road, Scott's hand still on her arm. "Have you heard of the Eagle Foundation?"

"They're a conservation group, aren't they?"

"Yes, that's right. I represent the northern Wisconsin region."

"I seem to recall you being active in environmental causes in college," Scott noted.

Abby giggled. It was a foolish, schoolgirl kind of giggle, and she immediately felt embarrassed, though the fact that Scott Frasier remembered *anything* about her made her giddy on a level she'd thought she'd left behind years ago.

Before she could make a bigger fool of herself, Scott's

head cocked to one side. He dropped her arm and took a step back in the direction they'd come.

Then Abby heard it—the distinct sound of a motor running, revving higher, much as the *Helene* had sounded when they'd first left the Bayfield pier. Concern immediately replaced embarrassment. "Is that our boat?"

"I believe so." Scott nodded and took a few more steps downhill.

Abby moved soundlessly toward him, listening carefully for some indication that would tell them what the boat, now hidden by thick trees, would be doing running its motor when Captain Sal had promised to wait for them.

"Perhaps he's just going around to the other side of the dock. Maybe it's a better spot there," Scott suggested.

Abby shook her head. "No chance of that. The west side of the dock is the only decent anchorage. On the east side the bottom is flat sandstone, which won't hold an anchor."

"You know the island pretty well." Scott sounded impressed as he picked up his pace and began to trot down the hill.

"I spent most of one summer living here while I worked for the Park Service." She just managed to keep up with him. A second later they cleared the edge of the trees, in time to see the *Helene* nosing for the gap between Rocky and Otter Islands.

"Hey!" Scott shouted, waving his arms in the air as he raced after the boat. "Hey, where are you going?"

He came to a stop near the end of the pier and Abby trotted up beside him, panting slightly, not just from the run, but from the oppressive fear she felt creeping up from her stomach to her lungs, its cold fingers gripping her, making it difficult to breathe. "He's leaving us." She could still see Captain Sal sitting at the wheel of the boat. He looked back twice and had to have seen them but made no move to communicate. Instead he hunched his shoulders, almost as though he was trying to shrink smaller and hide.

"Why would he do that?" Scott stared out in the direction the *Helene* had gone, though she'd soon be out of sight around Rocky's southern tip. "Do you think he forgot something? He said he'd give us two hours. It hasn't even been one."

Abby shook her head, the fear sending shivers up her arms. She'd never liked Devil's Island. It had only ever brought her trouble and heartache. And now she had a very bad feeling she was going to be spending far more time there than she ever would have wanted. "There isn't really anywhere he could go and be back in that short of time. I think he was just waiting for all of us to be out of sight before he left. It looks to me like he's headed back toward Bayfield but he doesn't want to be seen."

"So he's just leaving us here?" The *Helene* was out of sight now, and Scott turned back to Abby.

"That's what it looks like to me." As she spoke, Abby tried to push back her fear.

Scott didn't like the helpless feeling that crept over him when he saw his mother, Marilyn, picking her way back across the rocky shore toward the dock with Mitch beside her. He had no idea why Captain Sal had made off with the boat. At least Abby had some familiarity with the island. He could only hope she'd know how to get them back to the mainland.

As he could have predicted, his mother's face was blanched white by the time she reached the dock. "Please tell me he's coming back," she insisted.

"I don't know," Scott told her, though he had a pretty good idea, given the man's body language, that he'd purposely left them.

"Didn't he say he'd be back in two hours? We did say two hours, didn't we? Maybe he thought we said *ten* hours."

Before Scott could reply, Mitch barked, "Where's the boat?" He gave Scott a look as though he'd somehow been behind its disappearance.

"Somewhere south of here," Scott responded vaguely. His mom had been emotionally fragile ever since his father had died four years before. Scott knew the current situation would shake her even more. He wished he knew how to keep Mitch from making it worse.

"Why'd he take off? When's he coming back?" Mitch's face turned red from the combined effort of shouting and tromping down the dock. "Where's your mother's purse—and her diamonds?"

At the mention of his mother's jewelry, Scott spun around, taking in Marilyn's bare wrists and fingers in a single glance. He leveled his gaze at Mitch. "You left her jewelry on the boat?"

"Of course," the shorter man shot back. "The last time we visited an island, she lost her tennis bracelet. Did you think we were going to take a chance like that again?"

Scott wanted to shake his stepfather, or at least demand to know why his mother had worn the jewelry in the first place, but he didn't want to upset her further. She was already wringing her hands, and her face had gone as pale as the thickly clouded sky behind her.

Scott trained his attention on Mitch. "So you left all her jewelry on the boat, along with her purse, which contained…what? Credit cards? Cash? Checkbook?"

Marilyn nodded morosely. "And my cell phone, and the keys to the Escalade. Captain Sal said his lockbox was the safest place for valuables."

At the mention of the cell phone, Scott saw Abby pull hers from the slender canvas purse she wore strapped diagonally across her torso. She flipped it open, blinked at the screen, then made a face and shut it again. "No signal," she explained when she looked up and he caught her eye. "Didn't figure there would be. Reception's patchy enough in Bayfield, and that's over twenty miles from here."

As if on cue, Mitch checked his own phone. "Me neither."

Though he didn't expect much, Scott pulled out his phone, with the same result. "Fine." He exhaled loudly, then took a steadying breath and turned his attention to Abby, once again glad she was with them. "We need to get in touch with the authorities, get Mom's credit cards and checks stopped, tell them to keep an eye out for Captain Sal, and get somebody out here to pick us up. How do we do that?"

Abby looked from him to his distraught mother and back again, then spoke in a low voice. "There's a radio up at the old keeper's quarters. The place is probably locked up tight now that summer's over, but I think I can get us in." She put on bright smile and raised her voice, clearly for his mother's benefit. "The Coast Guard should be out to get us in a couple of hours. No problem. We'll be back in Bayfield in time for a late lunch."

Scott added an authoritative nod to back up her words, but his mother's eyes still looked haunted. "Hey, Mom." He put an arm around her shoulders, and she immediately crumpled against him. "It's okay. You just enjoy yourself, find some more driftwood. Everything will be taken care of. They'll have the police waiting for Sal the minute he gets into port. And did you hear what Abby said? We'll be back in Bayfield this afternoon. You start thinking about where you want to eat, okay?"

Marilyn sniffled and clung to him a moment longer. "I shouldn't have worn my jewelry. I should have left it all at home. But Mitch said it would be okay, that there's no point having jewelry if you don't wear it."

Scott didn't bother to give his opinion of Mitch's intelligence.

His mom finally took a step back and looked him in the eyes, her tears dissolving the otherwise impermeable black lines of makeup around her eyes. "Our accountant has all my credit card and bank information. Have the authorities get in touch with Kermit. His number is…" She pinched her temples and her voice wavered. "It's on my phone. In my purse."

Scott pulled her close again and pressed his lips to her forehead. "It's okay, Mom. Kermit Hendrickson, right? We'll just have them look him up. No big deal." He placed two steadying hands on her shoulders and took a step back. "Abby and I are going to go make that call. The sooner we do that, the sooner this is all going to get fixed. You'll be okay."

"Yes." Marilyn straightened and drew in a loud breath, then turned to face Abby. "Thank you for your help." She extended her hand. "I don't believe we've been introduced. I'm Marilyn Fra—" She stopped herself, cleared her throat. "Adams. Scott's mother. And this is my husband, Mitchell Adams."

Abby took Marilyn's hand and introduced herself, her expression kind but not pitying. "Thanks for letting me tag along with you guys today, by the way."

"Oh." Marilyn's face fell. "Well, let's hope you still feel

that way once all of this gets sorted out. I hope we haven't ruined your day."

"Nah." Abby dismissed her concerns. "I could use a little more excitement in my life." She smiled and turned to face Scott. "Ready?"

Scott checked with his mother once again to make sure she was okay with him leaving, and then headed back up the road with Abby. "Did you leave anything on the boat?" he asked once they were out of earshot of his mother.

"No." She gestured to her purse. "I've got everything I brought right here—not that I have much anyone would want, probably."

"I'm sorry we got you stuck out here. I guess Captain Sal couldn't resist the temptation of running off with all those diamonds. I don't understand whatever possessed my mom to leave them on the boat, or to wear them out on the lake in the first place."

"It sounded like Mitch thought it would be okay," Abby noted, walking carefully beside him. "Anyway, I don't know how much he'll get away with, but surely not enough to make up for his trouble. There's no way he'll get anywhere near Bayfield again, not without being arrested. It's not like a big city where people can slip in and out anonymously. Whatever business he had here will be over after a stunt like this."

Her comment piqued Scott's curiosity. "Is he well-known in this area?"

"I'd never seen him before today, but if the Park Service concessionaire recommended him to you guys, he has to have been around a while, or at least had legitimate references. I'm just saying it's a small town, and word travels fast. His reputation will be ruined."

Scott's steps slowed, but his heart rate picked up considerably. "The Park Service concessionaire," he repeated. "Did you find Captain Sal through the Park Service?"

"No. I was going to go by, but I thought I'd stop by the dock first to take a look at the lake and see how many boats were out, and whether anyone was in pier. Several of my friends have boats and I thought I might try to bum a ride with one of them if they were going out. None of them were around, but then I saw Captain Sal pulling in his For Hire sign."

Scott knew the rest. She'd come walking down the wharf just as they were about to head out, and she'd asked where they were headed. When they'd told her they were going out to Devil's Island, she'd asked to tag along. Mitch had frowned at the idea of another passenger, but his mother had been excited to have another woman aboard. Scott had cast the tie-breaking vote. Though he hadn't seen her since college, he'd always liked her easygoing personality and pretty face, and wasn't about to turn her away, especially since he hadn't been looking forward to spending the day with Mitch anyway. He'd told her to climb aboard. She hadn't hesitated.

But now her voice faltered. "You booked him through the concessionaire, didn't you?"

Scott stopped in his tracks. The road was getting steeper, which hampered their progress on the slippery path. He looked Abby full in the face as he admitted, "I don't know. My mom and Mitch are planning to drive around the Great Lakes to see the fall colors. They got a room in Bayfield last night, and I drove up from Saint Paul this morning. By the time I arrived, they'd already booked the boat."

"Did they mention—" Abby began, but Scott shook his head.

"They didn't say anything about it." At the look of trepidation that crossed her face, Scott wished he could tell her that Mitch would have done the right thing, but he really had no grounds for such assurances. In fact, in his experience, Mitch tended to get things wrong pretty consistently.

Abby seemed to understand. "If he wasn't booked through the Park Service, no one else may have a record on him." Her voice held steady as she explained the possibilities. "There are plenty of places he could go on this lake. He may not go back to Bayfield. He may not even be named Sal. In fact, it seems, just based on what we know of the situation, that the Captain didn't just fall prey to temptation. He may have planned on pulling a stunt like this, and just got lucky that your mom was so willing to leave her jewelry on board."

Her words articulated the vague fears Scott had felt ever since he'd seen the *Helene* speeding away from Devil's Island. But he took one of Abby's hands and squeezed it. "That's all the more reason why we need to get to that radio and alert the authorities promptly. The sooner they get after him, the better chance they have of catching him."

"Right." Abby pasted on a smile for him, but he could still see the fear in her sapphire-blue eyes and hear the slight tremble in her voice. "Let's get going, then."

They had to pick their way up the slimy road, and it was slow going. Abby nearly wiped out twice, so Scott didn't let go of her hand until they reached the keeper's quarters. The sturdy old whitewash and brownstone house looked solid, almost impenetrable.

But Abby seemed to know just what to do. She dropped his hand and immediately began tipping back the large fieldstones that encircled the autumn remains of a flower-bed at the front of the house.

"What are we looking for?" Scott decided to interject a little humor. "A trapdoor?"

"No." She gave him a chuckle that only sounded a little bit strained. Then she lifted another rock, plucked up a slender object from the earth, and announced triumphantly, "This."

Abby wiped the key on her jeans and took the front stairs two at a time, explaining, "Seems that once, many years ago, some Park Service staff came out here and forgot their key, then had to turn around and go all the way back to headquarters. They lost a full day's work. Ever since, there've been keys to just about everything hidden on each of the islands. You just have to know where to look." With that, she slid the key into the modern brass dead bolt and gave it a turn.

"I'm so glad you came along today." Scott bounded up the stairs after her and had to stop himself before he instinctively gave her a hug.

"Thank me after we're rescued, okay?" She barely glanced around before heading through the tomblike chill of the old house to the back kitchen.

Scott spotted the radio communications box on the counter just as Abby reached it and began flipping switches, waiting impatiently and then scowling when she didn't get a response.

"I don't understand," she muttered, flipping a toggle down and up again.

"I think I do." Scott reached past her to the lifeless power cord. He held up the severed end for her to see. "It's been cut."

TWO

"Cut?" Abby looked from the cord to Scott in disbelief. "But tampering with Park Service equipment is illegal. Who would do such a thing?"

The line of Scott's mouth was tense and white. "Perhaps the same person who would leave four people stranded on an island just so he could steal their jewelry and credit cards."

"No." Abby backed away, bracing herself against the counter for support. It didn't add up. "No, it's not worth it. I mean, I don't know how much your mom's jewelry is worth, or her credit cards, or— What did you say she drove?"

"An Escalade. Next year's model."

"Okay." Abby nodded. "So that's an expensive vehicle, but think about the risk. The Apostle Islands National Lakeshore is a national park. That makes his crime a federal offense. And leaving the four of us here, with no way to communicate with the mainland, with no way to get back…" The reality of their situation came crashing down on her in waves, and she crumpled back against the cupboards. "The temperatures get down well below freezing at night. We don't have any food, we don't have proper clothing. This island has wolves, foxes, bears—all kinds of dangerous animals. The tourist season was over weeks ago. No one's likely to come by here until after the spring thaw." She felt her eyes widen with realization as she lifted her head to look at him. "We could die out here."

"No." Scott shook his head and reached for her, his hand warm on her shoulder. "We'll get off the island. We'll be back in Bayfield this afternoon."

Abby wanted to believe him, but she knew the island too well. "How?"

She quickly saw that his words were empty hope.

"I don't know, but there has to be a way." He fingered the raw edge of the power cord. "Maybe we could splice this back together again." He tipped the machine over and looked at the back. "I'm sure whoever cut the cord took the backup battery, too."

"Wait." Abby headed to the far wall. "I thought of this just before you showed me the cord." She flipped the light switch into an upright position. Nothing happened. She flipped it back and forth a couple more times just to be sure, then headed to the refrigerator. The light didn't come on when she opened the fridge. She checked the freezer anyway, and found two full ice trays, which she pulled out and showed to Scott.

"Look," she said, staring down at the little rectangles of ice that floated in thawed puddles in each compartment. "This freezer had to have been running until recently. I wonder how long it would take the ice to thaw this much."

"In this weather, maybe a couple of days, maybe less, who knows? Either way, it looks like Captain Sal went to a lot of trouble to make sure we wouldn't be able to get that radio up and working." Scott took the ice trays from her and put them back in the freezer. He was apparently optimistic about getting the power back on.

That thought would have been enough to make Abby smile if it weren't for the cold dread she felt. She tried to shake the feeling. "Do you think it's just a weird coincidence?" she posited. "Captain Sal would have had to *know* somebody wanted to come out to *this* island, and that he'd be able to steal enough from them to make it worth his trouble. What are the odds of that?"

"What if he had prior knowledge my parents were coming out?" Scott challenged.

As Abby looked into Scott's face, his I-dare-you-to-deny-it expression made her wonder whose side he was on. But then his eyes crinkled into a smile and she dismissed her fear. "Would he have any way of knowing that?" she asked.

"Who knows? Mitch has always liked to run off at the mouth. He could have been blabbering about their plans all over town yesterday. Anyone could have overheard him and noticed how much jewelry my mom was wearing. I doubt it was some grand conspiracy." He shrugged. "We don't know why we've been left here. But it seems to me we're going to have to do something if we want to get off this island."

Abby agreed. "You're right. And we need to get back to your folks and let them know what's happening."

"No, Abby, wait." Scott's hand caught her shoulder, pulling her gently back toward him.

She looked up into his eyes, and for a second, she was a lovestruck freshman again, sitting in a desk next to the coolest guy in school, all too aware of how close she was to him.

"Please don't let on to my mother that anything is wrong. She's been through some tough times lately, and I don't think she can handle all the complexities of our current situation right now, at least not until we have a plan to get us out of here."

The moment he spoke the words, Abby realized Scott was exactly right. She'd seen how shaken Marilyn had been earlier, and the situation hadn't been nearly as frightening then. "I'm sorry." She bowed her head penitently. "I should have thought of that. We don't even know what we're up against, and it's not as though she's in any position to help. We need to examine our options."

"Right. What are our options?" He gave her a sheepish look. "You're the expert here. I've never even been to this island before."

Abby was tempted to ask why he'd come, but there wasn't time for chitchat. "Well, as far as I can see." She led him into the front room, where a huge mural of the islands covered one large wall. She reached up and put a finger on Devil's Island, the farthest north of the twenty-two Apostle Islands. "We've got three main options. One, we can get off this island by ourselves. Two, we could be rescued, either by contacting someone on the outside, or if we get really lucky, drawing the attention of a passing boat."

Scott looked impressed. "What are the chances we could draw the attention of a passing boat?"

Abby took a deep breath. "Have you seen any passing boats?"

"No."

"There are shipping channels six and twelve miles north of here, where the big ore ships travel. But they can hardly see the island from there. I mean, we could write *help* in driftwood on the beach, but there's no way they'd see it."

"What about airplanes?"

"Ditto. The only thing likely to come close would be a small sightseeing plane, but they're rare enough in the summer months. The tourist season is over for the winter, and most local pilots are just as wary as the boaters about going out this late in the season, anyway. Storms blow up quickly around here, often with very little warning, and getting caught in one out here tends to be deadly."

"What about a signal fire?"

Abby had to smile at Scott's creativity and persistence. "That would be a great idea, if it hadn't rained last night. Most of the wood around here is probably too soaked to burn. Besides, people burn campfires out on these islands all the time. Unless the fire was enormous, most people would just think it was a campfire, if they could see the smoke at all."

"So, you said we had three options. What was our third?"

Lowering her hand slowly from the map, Abby tried to remember. What had she been thinking? "Pray," she said finally in a soft voice.

"I guess we should be doing that anyway." Scott took both of her hands in his.

It took Abby a moment to grasp what he was doing.

By the time she'd realized he was serious, he'd closed his blue eyes and tipped his face up imploringly. "Dear Lord," he began, and only then did Abby come to her senses enough to snap her eyes shut and pray with him.

"We're in over our heads here, and we don't understand what's going on," Scott continued in a confessional tone. "This is way more than we can even begin to deal with, but we trust that You are watching over us, and providing whatever we will need. We need Your help. We need You to protect us throughout this ordeal that's before us, so we can live lives that are glorifying to You. In Jesus's name, Amen."

Abby kept her eyes shut a minute longer, her heart filled with wonder. In spite of the damp chill of the house, she felt oddly warm. She couldn't recall when she'd last prayed with another person, unless she counted the corporate prayers at church. For her, praying had always been a private thing, so private she rarely prayed aloud. When her eyes popped open, she realized a stray tear had escaped down her cheek.

"I'm sorry." Scott brushed it away with his thumb. "I guess I didn't even ask you if that was okay. I seemed to recall from college days that you were a Christian."

"Yes, I was. I am," Abby assured him, clearing her throat to raise her voice above a whisper. "I'm just feeling a little overwhelmed with everything." Like the ring in her pocket, and how Trevor would react if she didn't get it back to him. She straightened and pulled her hands free of his, the contact too lasting, too intimate, especially after the prayer. "You're used to praying with others, aren't you?"

"I do it all the time in my job as a Christian counselor, usually at the beginning and end of each session, and sometimes right in the middle, too."

"Ah." Abby had known he was some kind of psychologist. The Christian kind, apparently.

"I usually make sure my clients are comfortable with prayer before we pray together. I suppose I forgot my standard protocol, perhaps due to the strange setting, or because you still seem so familiar to me, even after all these years."

Abby felt herself blush. Scott remembered her. He remembered things about her. She found herself wishing they had more than just that morning to spend together before he went back to the Twin Cities. Then she remembered they were stuck on Devil's Island, and if they didn't figure out an escape plan soon, they might have far more time together than they'd planned on. But it wouldn't be pleasant.

She pointed at the island on the map again. "Here we are," she said, mostly to reorient herself. "The closest island is Rocky, two miles to the southeast. This time of year, both the wind and the waves tend to come from the west, so they'd be more or less in our favor if we headed that way, though we might have trouble keeping a southerly course." Reciting the facts long-ingrained in her mind helped her keep her thoughts off the way being around Scott made her feel.

"Are we thinking of heading out across the water?"

"Well, if we can't get someone to come to us, we've got to go to them." She looked at him for just a moment, decided he was still too distractingly attractive, and turned her attention back to the map. "The other choice would be to go with the waves due east to North Twin Island, but that's a good six miles or more. Depending on what we can round up for transportation, it might work in a pinch. Or we could end up there if we're unable to stay far enough south to make it to Rocky Island."

"But Devil's is the farthest island north. If we drift farther north, we'll miss landing anywhere."

Abby swallowed back a lump of fear and stuck to the comfort of physical facts. "The north shore of Lake Superior is about thirty miles from here. If we were able to man a seaworthy craft, and if we weren't intercepted by a vessel first, we'd end up there."

"In Canada?"

"Yes."

"What do you suppose are the odds of us coming up with a craft seaworthy enough to carry us all the way to Canada?"

"I can't say until we look."

Scott took a step closer, so close Abby could feel the

warmth radiating off him as he stood behind her and reverently touched the mural on the wall. His fingers moved just below hers, to the goose-necked shape of Rocky Island. "So this is our goal, hmm. Rocky Island? And what happens if we make it there? We hope the power hasn't been cut? We go island-hopping on to South Twin?"

Once again, the teasing-yet-practical tone of Scott's words caused Abby to smile, in spite of the seriousness of the situation in which they found themselves. "Unless something's changed recently, Rocky was always one of the few islands with a Park Ranger on duty year-round. There's a house on the far east side, on the low-lying flats on the other side of the forest-covered bluffs." She moved her hand to show which part of the island she was referring to, and brushed his fingers. "You can't see Devil's Island from that vantage point, so the Ranger's not likely to see any messages we try to write on the beach, or even spot any fires we make."

"But if we can get to the island," Scott said, his hand nestled close to her fingers.

"He'll be able to help us," she finished for him, trying to ignore the way the close contact of his fingertips made her thoughts skitter like so many leaves in the wind. She tried not to think about how close behind her he stood, though she knew if she so much as leaned back she'd be in his arms.

"All right." Scott's voice broke the spell as he nodded his head with an air of certainty and shoved his hands in the pockets of his jeans. "Now where are we going to find a seaworthy craft?"

Abby headed toward the door, retreating from the feelings she'd felt. "There are several outbuildings we can check. Who knows what might have been stashed out here over the years?" She fell back on words and action to keep herself from even considering what the emotions stirring in her heart might mean.

Abby locked the door behind them and returned the key to its hiding place before starting off toward the nearest outbuilding, a large shed not far from the house.

They couldn't find a key to the shed. Abby even ran back to the keeper's quarters and tried the key from under the rock, but the hole in the lock was too small. Finally she put her hands on her hips and stared at the building, trying to remember what had been inside when she'd worked on the island six years before. The insides of so many sheds and outbuildings ran together in her mind, and she couldn't sort it out. Somewhere, though, she had a vague recollection of having seen, here and there, aging rowboats, old fiberglass dinghies and all manner of historical marine artifacts that had been kept around for educational displays for the tourists who visited the islands in the summer months.

"We could try that little window," Scott suggested, pointing to the small wooden-shuttered opening above the main door.

Abby looked at Scott's broad shoulders and then looked back at the window. "It's ten feet in the air, and I don't think you'll fit through."

"But you can. Come on, I'll hoist you up."

A riot of protests filled Abby's mind, most of them involving the width of her hips, but Scott looked determined. Abby sighed. They had wasted plenty of time already looking for a key, and she felt desperation rising inside her.

She had less than thirty-six hours to get the ring back to Trevor. Every minute counted.

"Come on." Scott crouched low, his back braced against the door. "Stand on my shoulders."

"My hiking boots are going to hurt you," Abby warned him as she moved forward and pulled off her purse, tossing it to the ground before placing a tentative hand on his ball cap.

"I'll be fine. I'm made of pretty tough stuff," Scott assured her.

She hadn't been too worried about how tough he was—she'd been more embarrassed by the idea of such close contact with the man she'd always mooned after. Still, she realized his suggestion was a shrewd one, and relented. Stepping up on his knees, Abby somehow got both of her feet steady on Scott's shoulders. He held tight to her ankles as he stood, and then she cautiously straightened, crawling upward with her hands against the side of the building until she stood on eye level with the window. Grabbing tight to the sill with one hand, she lifted the old wooden lever-style latch and pulled the window open.

"Good news," she called down to Scott. "There's no glass."

"Great. Can you make it in?"

Though his words sounded steady, Abby was aware of how much pressure her shoes must be exerting on his shoulders. She tried to hurry.

"I think so." She dipped her head and shoulders inside, but most of her body still hung outside. "Mind if I step on your head?"

"Do what you've got to do."

Abby put most of her weight on her arms and pulled herself up, stepping on Scott's cap mostly for balance. She felt his hands change position on her ankles as he lifted her higher, supporting much of her weight with the sheer strength of his arms. She scrambled to pull herself through the window and was glad to find rafters within reach of the window sill so she wouldn't be forced to fall the entire ten feet to the floor.

Her hips wedged in the window, but she barely had time to consider the embarrassment of getting stuck there before she shifted sideways and pulled herself through. Then it was simply a matter of dropping to the floor and letting her eyes adjust to the darkness.

She tried the light switch. It was dead. Probably on the same line as the house, she reasoned. With the window open above her, enough overcast sunlight spilled in for her to identify a large lawn tractor, a workshop area, rusting old snow blower, sawhorses and gas cans.

"Are you all right in there?" Scott called.

"Yes," she answered back. Much as she wished she could tell him she'd found something, there was nothing in the shed that looked like it would float. As she stood there, she realized all the items were for the maintenance of the area around the keeper's quarters. Boats were more likely to be housed closer to the lake. Thanking God for at least providing her with a way out of the shed, she turned the dead bolt and stepped back out into the light.

Scott did what he could to help Abby with her quick search of the outbuildings, but his enthusiasm for the search began to wane quickly. As Abby scrambled around, peeking in windows when she couldn't find a key, he felt time and again the contrasting emotions of hope and disappointment as, in building after building, they came up with nothing.

"I don't want to sound pessimistic," he offered after Abby shut the door on the last building in the area of the keeper's quarters, "but wouldn't someone who'd gone to all the trouble of cutting off our electricity and cutting the line on our radio probably check to make sure they hadn't left us a boat?"

"I suppose so. But they may have overlooked something. This is still a pretty big island," Abby told him as they headed back down the road toward the dock. They'd both found decent walking sticks over the course of their searching, and with the extra limbs, were able to move a little faster down the slippery trail.

Scott was glad Abby was keeping a positive attitude. He only wished his mother could be so resilient. He'd hoped they'd at least be able to find a boat so she wouldn't be utterly crushed by the news they were unable to get in touch with the Coast Guard.

Apparently Abby was thinking along the same lines. "You know," she offered after they'd gone a couple hundred yards, "we'll have to tell your mother that we might not get rescued today. I know she's not going to like hearing it, but she'll probably take the news a lot better if we tell her while it's still daylight instead of waiting until it's cold and dark."

"You're right," Scott agreed morosely. He sighed, unsure how much of his mother's story Abby needed to hear in order to understand how to deal with his mom. "It's not that she's a flighty person by nature. For most of my life I considered her to be pretty hardy, actually. But four years ago, my dad went out hunting and didn't come back by suppertime. Mom knew something must be wrong, and she called me. I was living in Saint Paul, a good four-hour drive from home, so I couldn't be there. She went out, alone, and found him on some land my family owns. He was dead."

"Heart attack?" Abby asked, her voice concerned.

Scott shook his head. "Hunting accident." He paused on the trail.

"Oh, I'm so sorry." Abby came to a stop beside him, her face knit with empathy.

"His death was really hard for Mom to take. She's had a difficult time ever since."

"Financially?" Abby's voice sounded sympathetic.

"No." Scott thought her question seemed odd, especially given how many diamonds his mother had been wearing that morning. She didn't look like a woman down on her luck, by his estimation. "Why would you think that?"

Abby blushed bright red. "I'm sorry. That's horrible of me to ask. I just thought, well, since she and Mitch didn't seem to get along so well…" She put one hand up and covered her face in an embarrassed gesture.

Trying not to smile at Abby's embarrassment, Scott filled in the gaps. "You thought perhaps she'd married Mitch for his money."

At his words, Abby hid behind both her hands. "It sounds terrible when you say it that way. I shouldn't have even thought it, let alone said anything."

"No, I understand. It makes sense, and given all the trouble we've found ourselves in on account of my mother's diamonds, I'd say you have every right to ask about them. But those diamonds are about the only thing Mitch has ever given her, to my knowledge. He gave her several pieces of jewelry during their courtship, but since they married last summer he's been living off her wealth. The truth is, my father left my mother very well taken care of. Father had a large life insurance policy, besides his investments and our family home. And then there's always the family land."

"Land?"

"Our family owns a few square miles of virgin forest, which to my understanding is worth several million dollars, and could be vastly more valuable if properly developed."

Abby scrunched her face up. "Several million dollars, hmm? That sounds like a much better incentive than a vehicle and some diamonds."

"Yes," Scott agreed, "but it's *land*. It's not as though someone could easily get their hands on it."

"I suppose you're right," Abby agreed. "But there's still so much about what's happened today that doesn't add up." She took a deep breath and started moving down the trail again. "So, your mother inherited the land when your father died?"

"Not immediately. Father was my grandparents' heir. My grandfather had passed away the year before, but my grandmother was still alive at the time of Dad's death, though she'd been battling cancer for years. My grandfather's death was a horrible blow to her. When my father passed away, too, she pretty much gave up." As Scott reviewed his family history, he considered the idea that someone might be after the valuable land.

Clearly Abby was thinking similar thoughts. "You don't think it's possible someone would leave us out here in an effort to blackmail your mother into giving up the land?"

"It's possible someone might try it, yes," Scott acknowledged. "But my mother won't sell. That land is the Frasier family legacy."

"What do you mean?"

"I mean, when my mother dies, all the land will go to me."

THREE

Abby couldn't tear her eyes away from Scott's face. She didn't know him well enough to read him. All at once, she realized he was essentially a stranger, in spite of the long-ago connection they shared and the attraction she felt toward him. She remembered the sliver of doubt she'd felt earlier. And now he'd come right out and told her he was in line to receive millions of dollars worth of land as soon as his mother passed away. Was it any coincidence that Marilyn now found herself in a potentially life-threatening situation?

Had Scott brought his mother to Devil's Island to get Marilyn out of the picture so he could claim the land for himself? If so, Abby wondered why he'd confess everything to her. Had she, by joining in the boat trip today, unwittingly sentenced herself to death?

She shook off her fears in a shiver that traveled down the length of her spine. No, Scott was a Christian. He'd prayed with her. She couldn't believe he'd plot to kill his own mother. The whole idea was completely absurd. She needed to focus on getting off the island instead of letting the place spook her into inventing ghost stories out of nothing.

Scott's forehead furrowed thoughtfully beneath his Northwoods College ball cap. "What are you thinking?" he asked.

"I'm thinking you're starting to scare me." She tried to interject lightness into her voice, as though she found the idea more funny than frightening.

One corner of his mouth bent upward. "I'm guessing you don't scare easily."

"I don't." She forced a smile, then checked her watch. "Anyway, we need to get back to your mom and Mitch. It's already after noon, and the sun goes down by six o'clock these days. We should try to use whatever daylight we have left to get ourselves off this island, or at least make preparations for keeping warm tonight."

"Then we'd better get moving."

Not daring to move any faster on the slick trail even with her walking stick, Abby just managed to keep up with Scott's long strides. She still felt distinctly uneasy about being stuck on the island, and was no longer as comfortable as she'd felt earlier about being marooned there with Scott. Her top priority was to get back to Bayfield.

They cleared the last of the trees and the dock fell into view. Sure enough, there was nothing on either side but water. Abby felt her heart sink just a little more. She hadn't expected Captain Sal to come back for them, but she realized upon seeing the empty dock, that a part of her had dared to hope there had been some innocent reason for his abrupt departure, and that they hadn't actually been abandoned at all.

No chance of that now, so Abby dismissed the thought. Instead she focused on what they would tell Marilyn, who was sitting cross-legged on the dock between Mitch and a large pile of driftwood.

Leaning closer to Scott, Abby told him in a hushed voice, "I have an idea about what to do with your mom."

At the same time, she unzipped her purse and rifled through its scant contents.

"What's that?"

She found the little white dispenser she'd been looking for and pulled it out triumphantly. "We need to give her something to do so she won't feel so helpless."

"Good idea." He looked at the object in her hands. "Floss? We're going to distract her with dental hygiene?"

Abby threw her head back and laughed at Scott's teasing suggestion. She was glad he was able to keep his sense of humor in spite of their circumstances. "No, silly, we're going to ask her to go fishing."

At the sound of her laughter, Mitch and Marilyn turned their heads. Marilyn jumped up and trotted up the hill to meet them, her face bright. "Well, how soon are they going to get here? I've decided where we should go for lunch."

Scott put a hand on his mother's shoulder. "We might not make it back in time for lunch," he said, breaking the news in a voice buoyed by hope, "but we're working on it. In the meantime, we've got a project for you and Mitch."

As Scott outlined the plan, Abby tied long lengths of floss securely to each walking stick, using the large knots in the wood as a brace to keep the string from slipping off. Marilyn seemed eager to help, especially once Scott explained it was up to her to fish for their supper. Abby felt relieved the older woman was willing to rise to the challenge.

"You're going to need lures and hooks," Marilyn noted, handing over two brilliant diamond earrings.

"Oh, no, not your diamond jewelry," Abby refused.

But Marilyn was insistent. "Captain Sal got the rest of it. Honestly, I'd rather these go in the stomach of a fish than into the hands of a sneaky crook."

Abby looked at Scott's mom and realized she wasn't going to back down. "Well," she agreed hesitantly, "I guess these would work remarkably well. And we don't really have anything else." She felt a twinge of guilt at having Marilyn give so generously to the cause, when in reality the whole fishing bit had only been meant to distract her. But maybe Marilyn felt the need to compensate for her role in their being marooned in the first place.

The earrings had a French hook in back, with three dangling gems of graduated size. They'd be perfect as lures—as perfect as any diamond earrings could be, Abby figured. She knotted the floss several times over to insure they wouldn't be lost.

While she worked, she observed Scott and Mitch engaged in a hushed conversation farther down the dock. She promptly silenced her imagination when she found herself wondering if Scott and Mitch might be conspiring together. Instead she handed the makeshift poles to Marilyn with words of encouragement and headed over to the men.

"Oh, come on," Mitch said as she approached. "A strong guy like you? That can't be more than a mile or two. I used to swim that much all the time when I was your age."

Seeing where the older man pointed, Abby realized what he was suggesting.

"I really don't think it would be wise to try." Scott shook his head. "With the temperatures of these waters, a person could get into deep trouble in a hurry."

"Are you suggesting Scott attempt to *swim* to another island?" Abby asked as she approached them.

"Sure! Why not? That island there is pretty close. Scott was a college athlete. I think he's still got it in him."

"No," Abby informed them insistently, "it's not humanly

possible. The average temperatures of these waters are less than fifty degrees, even at the surface on a sunny day. Even with a life preserver, it's unlikely the strongest of swimmers would make it as much as a mile before succumbing to hypothermia. Rocky Island is two miles from here. Scott would die before he got halfway there." Abby recited the facts as she had so many times when she'd worked for the Park Service. Everyone seemed to underestimate the deadliness of the frigid waters. Far too often, it turned out to be a fatal mistake.

Mitch clearly didn't appreciate being corrected. "The waves are going that direction," he pointed out, "they'd practically carry him there. And I'm sure the surface water isn't nearly as chilly as the deeper parts of the lake. Why, we've gone swimming in Lake Superior before and had a very pleasant time."

Abby realized she'd touched a nerve, and possibly embarrassed him. She placed a gentle hand on his arm. "Look, it's a good idea. If this were a protected cove, and if the wind had been pushing warm surface water into a pool here, I'm sure Scott would have no problem swimming two miles. But this water is coming in from the open sea, where it's constantly turned over from the cold water in the depths. It's just not safe."

In spite of her calm tone, Mitch pulled his arm away, clearly offended. "What other options do we have? Given the circumstances, I don't think it's too much to ask Scott to risk it."

"And given the circumstances—" Abby met the man's eyes and did her best to stare him levelly down "—it wouldn't be a matter of *risk*. Striking out for Rocky Island as a swimmer would be suicide." She let out a frustrated breath and tried to calm her agitated nerves. She didn't like Mitch, and could understand why Scott had expressed a desire to avoid him. "Now, Marilyn is already doing her part by fishing to get us some supper. We have two poles. Why don't you join her?"

With a little more cajoling, Mitch reluctantly agreed. Then she and Scott headed up the shoreline to the two ancient boathouses half-hidden among the boulders farther up the shore.

They found the canoe up in the rafters of the second boathouse. Scott regarded it with disgust. "I'm not so sure this thing is puddle-worthy, let alone seaworthy." He assessed the ancient birchbark boat once they'd hefted it to the ground.

"If someone really did leave us here to die, it's quite possible they left this here thinking we'd take it into the open water and drown," Abby offered, then grinned at him. "But if so, then they seriously underestimated how seaworthy this kind of vessel can be. I believe this was once used as part of an educational display, but before that, it was built to be a functional canoe." She lifted one of the single-bladed paddles from the bottom of the boat. "We've got everything we need. I say we use it."

Scott's eyes narrowed. He wondered how Abby could possibly be serious. "You mean you would actually consider taking *this* boat out onto *that* lake?" He pointed at the choppy waves just beyond them.

"Not if I had a better option." Abby met his eyes. "Why don't we take it down to the dock and put it in the water? We can stay close to shore for a while and see how she holds up before we venture out very far."

Given their lack of alternatives, Scott decided Abby's suggestion sounded fair. She seemed to know plenty about the islands, and had the facts behind her to keep Mitch off his case. If he had to choose, he'd rather try the canoe than strike out for Rocky Island swimming. "Do you have much experience canoeing?"

"Not on the open sea," Abby admitted, "but I think I can manage not to tip us over, if that's what you're worried about."

Scott appreciated her scrappy attitude, and realized he probably sounded like he was whining. The problem was, he felt responsible for everyone else's safety, and he especially didn't like the idea of putting Abby at risk by letting her join him out on the water. But he also realized the two-person canoe would be nearly useless to him if he tried to man it himself.

"Okay, let's see what this relic can do," he agreed, meeting Abby's eyes and sensing apprehension there. So, she felt nervous, too. "I'm going to look for a bucket or something to bail with before we go, though. Even if this thing holds water, it's not enclosed like a kayak. If we get into some high waves, we could be swamped in a hurry."

"So you think we should try it?" Abby's voice sounded less certain now that Scott had agreed to her plan.

Scott crouched down and ran his fingers slowly over the smooth brown birchbark stretched tight across the wooden frame. The boat seemed so fragile, almost paper-thin, and so old. Would they be crazy to take it out on the lake? What if they got far from shore and ran into trouble? Worse yet, what if the waves pushed them out past the islands, into the open sea? There was no way the antiquated craft would make it to the shore of Canada. He looked up at Abby. "What are our other options?"

Abby looked around uneasily. Scott could see their precarious situation was starting to weigh on her. She hunkered down next to him and sat on the cement floor of the boathouse. "Does anybody know you're out here today?"

Her question made sense. How long would it be before anyone missed them, and would they know where to look for them even then? "I went out with some of the guys from work to celebrate my birthday last night," he explained. "I told them Mitch and my mom wanted to take me to another island today. I've visited seventeen of the islands, and Mitch has gotten it into his head that I need to eventually visit all of them. So they know I'm out here, but they don't know which island."

"And they expect you back at work on Monday?"

Uneasiness stirred in his stomach. "Actually—" Scott swallowed, trying to force down the fear that rose in his throat "—no. I'd planned to be back in the office Monday, but the guys said I'd been working too hard lately and had too much vacation time racked up. They told me to take some more time off and spend the week out here. I wasn't planning on it, but if I don't show up on Monday, they'll probably assume I've come to my senses and followed their advice for once."

"And your folks were planning to drive the circle tour around Lake Superior?" Abby clarified. "Do they tend to check in with anyone regularly?"

Scott shook his head. "I doubt it. I suppose they've got hotel reservations here or there, but people don't show up for reservations all the time. No one would raise an eyebrow." The facts were stacked against anyone coming looking for them, and Scott didn't like it. "What about you, Abby? How long would it take before anyone came out here looking for you?"

* * *

Abby froze. She could feel the cold of the cement boat-house floor seeping in through her legs, into her bones. So much had gone wrong on this trip. At Scott's question, her fears about his reason for being on the island resurfaced. No one knew she was there. But did she dare admit as much to him?

"I don't know," she admitted cautiously. "I have a lot of coworkers at the Eagle Foundation." She took a shaky breath and avoided his eyes. True, she had lots of coworkers, but they all telecommuted. She was the only one living in the Bayfield area. And though she tended to keep in touch regularly via e-mail, she'd had problems with her Internet connection in the past and been out of touch for days at a time. If no one heard from her for a week, they likely wouldn't be too concerned. And all of her family lived in the Chicago area. Though she kept in close touch, she'd sometimes gone a week or more without contact. Likely they wouldn't be alarmed if they didn't hear from her for that long.

After a long pause, Scott probed further. "Do you think any of them would miss you? Does anyone know where you are today?"

What would happen if she told him the truth? Had Scott brought his mother to the island with evil intentions? And if so, why had he agreed to let her come along? Abby prayed silently in her heart, and felt her pulse rate still. She glanced at the boat, and realized there was no way she'd be able to paddle the lengthy craft on her own. If she was going to get off the island, she had to trust Scott—with the truth, and with her life.

"Nobody knows I'm here," she admitted in a tiny

whisper. "No one will miss me for several days, and even when they do, they won't know where to look." She stared at his face as she spoke, hoping for some sign of whether he felt relieved or worried by her admission.

Scott's brow scrunched ever so slightly under the brim of his ball cap. Whether that was a good sign or bad, Abby wasn't sure. She looked at the orange-brown wood of the boat, and then to the gray-blue sea. "What do you think? Should we risk it, or wait for help to come to us? We could always wait a few days and then try the canoe."

"If we wait for help, we'll only become weaker. We don't have any food, we don't have any source of heat, one of us could be injured at any time, and as you said yourself, storms blow up here with little warning. If we wait too long, we might not be *able* to try the canoe. Our best shot with this thing is to try it right now, before we get any more tired and hungry, before the weather changes and before it gets too close to sundown. After all, once we make it to Rocky Island, we still have to find the Ranger Station on the other side of the island. We don't want to be wandering around in the woods in the dark."

His arguments made sense, but Abby still felt so uncertain. She closed her eyes and began to pray silently again. But before she'd hardly started, Scott spoke.

"Do you want to pray about it?" He reached for her hand.

She nodded. It almost felt natural holding Scott's hand, hearing him praying to God for wisdom and protection. Scott concluded the prayer, and Abby jumped up and brushed dust from the floor off of the back of her pants. "Thank you for praying. I think you're right. We should try the canoe."

"You really think so?"

"I do."

"Okay. Let me find something to bail with." Scott scavenged around until he found an old plastic bucket that had clearly been a child's sand toy, but was now faded and cracked. "This probably washed up on shore here, or someone left it behind, but it should work for what we need."

"Perfect," Abby agreed. "Now, let's get his canoe down to the dock and see if she holds water."

They hoisted up the canoe and found it to be more cumbersome than heavy. After walking a couple of minutes and making little progress with the canoe impeding each step, they lowered it to the ground and Scott suggested, "Why don't I just carry it over my head?"

"Can I help you?"

"I think it would be easier if I just did it myself."

Abby stood back as he hoisted the boat up over his shoulders and above his head.

"Have you got it? Are you sure you don't want me to help?"

"I'm fine." Scott took a few awkward steps toward the dock, then quickly found his rhythm and increased his pace. "It's much easier this way," he explained, his voice only slightly strained from effort, "and I'm afraid you're enough shorter than I am that it would make it more difficult if we both carried it than if I just do it by myself. Besides, you'll need to save your arm strength for paddling."

Abby understood his reasoning, but she couldn't help thinking he was carrying a heavier burden than he needed to. Still, she had to admit he was moving much faster with the canoe on his own than when she'd been trying to help him carry it.

Marilyn and Mitch pulled in their poles as Scott and Abby approached.

"You found a boat?" Marilyn asked with excitement.

Mitch looked wary. "Will that thing even float? It looks like it's a hundred years old."

"Look at it this way, Mitch," Scott huffed once he'd lowered the canoe onto the soft sand. "If the canoe doesn't get us to the next island, then I can try your idea of swimming for it."

At the incredulous expression on Mitch's face, Abby couldn't resist chiming in. "Really, the canoe only has to get us halfway there," she explained in a mock-serious voice. "Once we get within a mile of the island, we can swim for it."

"Oh, I think the water is awfully cold for that." Marilyn shuddered.

Abby knew she was right, but she didn't amend her statement. If anything happened to them in the water, Marilyn would be less concerned if she thought Abby and Scott had been prepared to swim for it.

"Well, I'm not going anywhere in that thing," Mitch insisted.

"I don't expect you to," Scott explained. "Abby and I are just going to take it over to Rocky Island. There's a Park Ranger stationed there, and he can call for help to come and get you two. This canoe is really only meant to hold two people, and I'd rather not have Mom out on the lake if we have to swim for it after all." He announced their plans with an air of finality, and then scooted the canoe into the water next to the dock.

"Abby, do you have any more of that floss to tie our bucket to the canoe?" he asked. "I don't want to lose it once we get out on the lake."

"I used it all on the fishing poles," Abby called after

him. The floss had been a small sample from her dentist she hadn't bothered to take out of her purse after her last appointment.

Marilyn handed Abby the two fishing poles. "Here. We won't need these anymore."

The waxed floss had already started unraveling from the knots she'd used to tie the earring lures in place. Abby quickly slid the slick string back and pulled the earrings free. "You'll want these back," she said, handing them over.

"No, really." Marilyn crossed her arms over her chest, rubbing her shoulders as though to comfort herself. "I'd rather not."

Unsure whether the woman's impulse had to do with regret at leaving the other gems aboard the *Helene,* or if Marilyn simply didn't want part of her jewelry without the rest, Abby decided not to push her, given her emotionally fragile state. She shoved the earrings deep into her back pocket for safekeeping, and realized at the same time she was acquiring quite a bit of jewelry in her pockets. After all, she still had the ring in the pocket at her hip, its tiny prick a sharp reminder of all that still lay before her.

Scott stepped over and gave his mother a hug goodbye before tying the bucket to a cross brace near the rear of the canoe. "Okay, let's see if she'll hold us."

Abby relented to being lowered in with Scott's help. He'd pulled the canoe to the end of the dock where the water was deepest, and she felt the boat dip precariously with her weight. But as she crouched at her place toward the front of the canoe, the mad rocking eased quickly. "Your turn," she called back to Scott.

There were no seats, so she sat on her knees and grabbed the sides while Scott lowered himself gingerly into place at the rear of the boat. Then he tossed a paddle to her. "Let's see what she can do."

They paddled free of the dock, gliding along easily as they moved into open water. Abby breathed deeply of the sea-scented air and tried to tell herself to enjoy their excursion. After all, when would she have an opportunity like this again? She was canoeing with Scott Frasier, something she'd have only dreamed about doing years before. But when she let out a shaky breath and dipped her paddle in the water again, she found she couldn't fight back her fear over the great risk they were taking.

"What do you think?" she asked, looking back and seeing no water in the bottom of the boat. "Does she look seaworthy?"

"I'd say so. And it occurred to me that we should probably make tracks before she changes her mind, don't you think? No point paddling around in the shallows and waiting for her to spring a leak."

Abby took a deep breath, her silent prayer little more than a mantra. *I will not fear, for Thou art with me.* She repeated the lines from the twenty-third Psalm over and over in her head and tried her best to believe them. "Okay," she agreed, digging deep with her paddle and feeling the canoe glide forward smoothly as a result. "Let's aim for the south end of Rocky. These waves are going to try to push us out to sea, and I'd like to do whatever I can to avoid that."

"Agreed. Pull hard on the left," Scott instructed, then shouted a goodbye to his mother, who waved before crossing her arms and hugging herself again.

For the next several minutes they paddled in relative silence, breaking the stillness only with the occasional, "keep her steady," or "harder on the left, I think we're drifting." But as they moved farther out from the protection of Devil's Island, the wind picked up and the waves began to get higher, lapping ever closer to the rim of the boat. At the same time, the lake seemed intent on moving them straight north, out into the open sea, and Abby found herself exerting more effort in keeping them steered in the right direction than she did in moving them forward at all.

"How are we doing?" she called back, glancing over her shoulder just long enough to see the autumn-clad form of Devil's Island looming behind them much closer than she'd have liked.

"We're making headway. Slow but steady. How are your arms holding up?"

"I'm doing fine. I'll probably be sore tomorrow, though. How are your arms? You already carried this canoe down the hill—you've got to be getting tired."

"I'm fine. I haven't gone as soft as Mitch would like you to believe."

Abby heard the strain behind his lighthearted words, and she dug a little deeper with her paddle, wincing as the seasoned wood moved against the skin of her palms where blisters had already begun to form. She tried to adjust her grip to ease the pain, but with the next dig, she still felt it. Rather than focus on her pain, she resolved to keep her eyes on their elusively distant goal.

"Harder on the left if you can," Scott called from behind her. His voice rose in pitch, his tension more obvious now. The waves splashed higher, jolting their boat and limiting their progress, sending the fragile craft rocking unsteadily. Abby wished she could find the rhythm of the waves and move with the water, but she feared the only way to do that would be to go with the direction of the waves and head

out to sea. And there was no way she was going to intentionally head out to sea.

"Steady now. If you can, I want you to paddle with
smaller, faster motions for a minute here while I try to bail
out some of this water."

Water? Abby looked behind her and saw five or six inches
of water pooled just beyond the toes of her boots, hampering their progress and holding them lower, inviting more
water to slosh in. She could feel the rush of adrenaline hit
her veins as she did her best to follow Scott's instructions.

Without the second paddler, the boat nearly stilled on
the lake. Abby wondered if they were even moving forward
at all. "How far do you think we've gone?" she called
behind her. "Are we halfway yet?"

She could hear Scott dumping water into the lake—
either that, or it was the splash of water coming in over the
side of the canoe. Since they were headed nearly straight
south, the westward-moving waves slapped them square on
the side, spilling into the boat as often as not. Abby bent
her head around and looked behind her.

Scott's face grimaced with pain as he plucked up his
paddle and dug deep, propelling the little boat forward—
by feet now instead of inches. "We're moving forward," he
grunted, "we're not turning back now."

But Devil's Island still loomed closer than Rocky. Abby
set her jaw and paddled harder. Scott was right. They
weren't going to turn back. There was nothing for them
back there, and they were just as likely to run into trouble
on their way back as forward. They might not be any closer
to Rocky than Devil's, but somewhere along the line,
they'd passed the point of no return.

The wind and waves mounted higher against them.

When Abby looked to the sky, she realized the gray clouds had grown dark and threatening, and the brisk breeze they'd been experiencing all day had blown up a gale that threatened to propel them into the open sea. As the boat lurched in the raucous waves, Abby's stomach somersaulted up her throat.

Water splashed into the boat in waves instead of rivulets. The puddle in their vessel grew and the tiny craft settled deeper into the lake, its sides lower, an easier target for the surf that seemed intent on swamping them. Abby paddled in near-frantic terror, but still she felt the boat stall whenever Scott paused to bail out the water.

Slowly they crept forward. As they drew closer to Rocky Island, Abby could see the waves sending up spray as they smacked against the huge boulders that gave Rocky Island its name. The thought hit her like a slap of cold lake water. Somehow, they'd have to navigate through the dangerous rocks in order to get to the island.

The Lord is my shepherd, I shall not want. Abby recited the words in her head, finding a rhythm with them, digging deep with her paddle and forcing herself to ignore the blisters growing on her palms. She wished she'd thought to tie her paddle to the boat, but it was too late now, and she wasn't about to shift her hands too much for fear of losing her oar to the lake.

The wind ripped the hood from her head and tore her hair free from the braid where she'd bound it, sending long strands of her dark locks flinging to her face, covering her eyes. She shook them free, only to have them flung at her again.

"I'm going to bail again," Scott called, and Abby switched her paddling pattern, feeling the muscles in her shoulders tighten into knots with the quicker, shallow movements.

It seemed like an eternity later when he shouted to her again. "Okay, dig deep now. We're getting closer. We're really getting closer."

And they were. Already Abby could see massive red stones hiding under the surface of the clear water, and had felt the thin underside of the boat bump against them more than once as the waves peeled back, revealing the menacing boulders lying in wait to tip them, or to smash their tiny boat to bits.

"Paddle harder. Paddle harder," Scott called, as Abby's strength sagged and fat tears rolled down her cheeks from the pain in her shoulders and hands. She *had* to paddle harder. She didn't have a choice. They were still several hundred yards from shore.

The bumps came more frequently now. At any time, they could hit a rock hard enough to crack a massive hole in their boat. Abby kept praying, kept digging, and nearly screamed when she felt the numbing water slosh against her legs.

She looked back. The middle of the canoe held nearly a foot of water! "Don't you want to bail?" she nearly screamed, as the wind ripped the words from her mouth and carried them away. The sky had grown more sinister, the tempest violent.

"Too late for that now. We're almost there. Just dig!"

Abby dug, tears spilling unchecked down her cheeks, mixing with the sea spray and the waves. The water sloshed higher, clenching its frozen fingers around her legs, sending searing pain through her bones from the fierce cold. The boat was so low in the water. So low, and so cold.

The red domes of the boulders poked their moss-streaked heads from the water like vicious trolls intent on sinking them. As each wave pulled back, another menacing boulder would leer up at them before the next wave sent them sloshing over its skull, the flexible birch yielding to the pressure, nearly folding, threatening to snap.

Three hundred yards. Two hundred. Abby could see the trees, the red bluffs and the rocky shore, before the wind whipped her hair into her eyes, blocking her view, blinding her to anything but the ice-cold water and the fear.

She never saw the boulder that tipped them. All she knew was that one moment, her muscles were in tight knots of effort, and the next, her whole body was thrown into the frigid lake and the water closed over her head.

FOUR

Instantly numb shock gripped her. It was all Abby could do to struggle upward, willing her frozen limbs to move against the churning waters, her face straining for the surface, seeking light, seeking air. She felt something move against her back and in her confusion, didn't recognize Scott's arms until he'd lifted her head and shoulders above the waves.

The brush of his hands felt foreign as he pulled the hair back from her face. Abby watched his mouth open and close. He was shouting something, but she couldn't hear any words. The sky blurred, the world tilted, then her ears started to work again, and she heard him.

"Run! You've got to get moving or you'll freeze to death. Run, Abby! Come on, we've got to get moving."

She didn't know how she made her legs move forward. She could hardly feel her feet as they slipped and slid across the submerged boulders, angry spears of pain the only reminder that she had feet at all. Scott's arm held her steady, lifting her, pulling her, his voice constantly urging her on. "Move, Abby, you've got to keep moving."

They stumbled forward, her stiff fingers no help as they grasped at seaweed, her shins and legs knocking against the rocks, falling, bruising, rising again. And always,

Scott's voice in her ear, "Keep going, Abby, you can do it, we're getting there, up you go, keep moving."

Then the water reached only to her waist and she moved more freely without the bashing waves to push her down. She stumbled onward, desperate to get out of the lake and away from the sneaky boulders that tripped her up and bruised her frozen muscles.

Soon the waves slammed in impotent fury against their feet, and then they were free of the sea. Abby's hiking boots were deadweights, her feet leaden blocks, as she scrambled forward up the jagged coast toward the woods.

"Keep running, keep moving," Scott urged her on. "Which way is it to the Ranger's house?"

Abby looked up and down, her mind slowly processing their position. "East," her voice slurred as her tongue froze in her mouth. She pointed, watching her hand as though it belonged to someone else, unable to feel anything more than the prickles of pain her movement prompted. "That way. We'll come to a road, it's at the end of the road. East. No, north." She moved her hand. "That way."

"Okay, let's keep going. You've got to keep moving."

Abby tried. The twenty-third Psalm was stuck in her head, running on constant replay, and her heart yearned for the still waters, the green pastures, anything but these deeply shadowed woods and these winds, which whipped through the dying autumn trees, flinging the last flaming leaves to the ground with fury and sending them scrambling across the forest floor.

She moved forward, willing her body to run, straining against the bile that rose in her throat and burned her lungs. Rocks and branches leaped up from nowhere in the pathless woods, tripping her, slamming against her with jarring force. Only Scott's strong arm around her kept her from falling face-first into the mud.

"Come on, Abby. Can you move faster? We've got to keep going." His voice echoed in her ears, caught in her head, tangled with the Psalm and the pain. Wasn't she moving? She told her body to move but she couldn't feel it anymore, couldn't feel anything but the cold and the heaviness of her sodden clothes that hung from her body and dragged her down.

"Abby?" Scott's hands were on her face, his eyes peering into hers with concern. She wanted to smile, to tell him she was okay. She opened her mouth. No words came out.

Scott snapped his fingers near her face. She was vaguely aware of the motion, the sound, but she didn't flinch. She couldn't.

"Abby!" His voice grow more insistent. "Can you hear me? Come on, Abby!"

She looked at him, begging him with her eyes, wanting to cry out for help. He seemed to be so far away, as though she was stuck at the bottom of a deep pit looking up at him.

And then his lips were on hers, warm lips, stealing the cold breath away and melting the frozenness that gripped her. When he pulled away, she smiled drowsily and his face came into focus.

"Can you go on?"

Her head felt heavy as she nodded, and she scrambled forward, leaning most of her weight on him, unsure how much she actually propelled herself forward and how much he simply carried her.

After tripping and stumbling so many times, she hardly noticed falling over a large branch until her face planted hard against the cold earth. The air whooshed from her lungs and she lay still for one long moment before she gathered the strength to inhale.

Scott lifted her again. His breath felt warm against her cheek. "I'm going to carry you," he explained as he hoisted her into his arms. Abby didn't protest, but held on as tightly as her frozen hands could manage. They lurched together as he moved across the uneven ground, and she burrowed her face against his strong shoulder, thrilling at the feel of his warmth against her cheek. Her last conscious thought was of green pastures.

Scott moved as quickly as he could through the dense forest, ducking branches, dodging boulders, picking his way in what he hoped was an easterly-northerly direction, or wherever Abby had pointed. Poor thing. He had to get her to the Ranger's house before her body temperature dropped any further. What was it he'd learned so many years ago in biology? Once the body's temperature dropped twenty degrees, it started shutting down. After that, there would be nothing he could do for her. Death would soon follow.

With that thought spurring him on, he picked up his pace as much as he could, running mostly on fear and will-power. He'd taken a pretty bad dunking, too, though his head had never gone underwater as Abby's had. He'd seen the boulder just before they'd hit it, had leaped free as the wave snapped their canoe like a match. The freezing waters had been enough of a shock to his system, and he was substantially bigger than Abby. Her smaller form had been quickly overcome by the cold. He was impressed she'd made it as far as she had before passing out.

But even now, he wasn't sure she was completely unconscious, though her arms hung slack and she slumped like deadweight against him. He could feel her breath tickling his neck, caught whispers of the words she murmured. "Though I walk through the valley of the shadow…Thou art with me."

His heart swelled. She was such a sweet girl, and she'd given it all she had. He couldn't fail her, he wouldn't, though his legs trembled now with every step. The sky grew darker, the wind more furious, but he stumbled on.

Scott didn't know how long he'd been following the road before he realized he was no longer tripping over rocks. The way was smoother here, though still a little uneven and washed out in places. Was he headed in the right direction? He prayed so.

The house appeared out of nowhere. A light shined in the window on the second floor. Scott gripped Abby's still form more tightly and ran toward it, his legs shaking as he climbed the porch steps. When he pressed the doorbell, he heard the chime echo through the house, and a moment later curious eyes peered out at him.

The door opened and he all but fell inside, warm air hitting his face like scalding steam. Two figures pulled him farther into the house.

"She took a dunking," he started to explain, but the woman, who wore a green Park Ranger's uniform just like the man's, was already tugging at his sleeve, pulling him down the hall.

"We've got to get her into the tub, got to get her warmed up in a hurry. Is she conscious?"

"Partly. I think." Scott sat Abby on the lid of the commode and started working loose the swollen laces of her hiking boots while the woman ran water in the tub.

"It takes a minute for the hot water to push through the

pipes," she explained, then addressed the old man who hovered in the doorway. "Get the space heater from the front room, Burt. And grab some more towels!" Deciding the temperature was warm enough, she plugged the drain.

Scott tugged off one hiking boot, then the other. His fingers felt stiff and useless against the clinging fabric of Abby's socks.

"Just stick her in the tub, clothes and all," the old woman commanded. "It'll be just as easy to get her clothes off in there."

Her suggestion made sense to Scott and he lifted Abby again, plunking her into the tub, surprised when she sat upright of her own accord and opened her eyes. "You still with us?" he asked, sliding her socks off and dipping her feet in the inch or two of water that had accumulated. Its warmth burned against his frozen fingers, but he didn't flinch. It felt good.

Abby looked at him and he watched her face blossom into a smile.

"It's warm," she whispered, beaming at him.

He returned her dopey grin but couldn't think of anything intelligible to say. Instead he gripped her bare foot with one hand and patted it with another, grateful she was alive, grateful to have delivered her so far. Emotions swirled within him like the steaming water that filled the tub, rising upward in a wordless prayer of thanks.

The old woman unzipped Abby's jacket and pulled her arms free while Burt returned with the space heater. She shooed both men out of the room. "You two get. This guy looks like he could use a bath, too." She pointed at Scott and closed the door on them.

Scott followed the old man up the stairs to another

bathroom, but didn't let him so much as turn on the water before explaining, "My family was marooned on Devil's Island. Could you please get in touch with the Coast Guard and have them send a boat over there to pick up my mother and stepdad?"

"Well, I'll see what I can do," the man said, his weathered face looking concerned, "but there's a pretty rough squall blowing up out there. Might take them a while to get out there."

"Then please, hurry, make the call. I can run my own bath. We need to get help over there as soon as possible." Scott didn't bother to try to mask his fear. He wouldn't leave his mother out there, not with a storm blowing up. "My mother's life may be in danger."

Abby floated in the blissfully warm water and dipped her head back until only her face broke the surface. The warmth seeped into her bones, slowly easing the dull cold ache from her marrow. Her fingers and toes tingled with delightful prickles that were almost painful, but Abby didn't care. She could finally feel her feet again. She was alive.

"Praise the Lord," she said aloud, then gulped in a mouthful of warm, sweet water, letting it run over and between her teeth, which had finally stopped chattering.

The knock at the door startled her.

"It's just me," called the woman who'd introduced herself as Elda. She opened the door and set a pile of clothes on the commode. "These might be a little big, but they're dry. Should work."

"Thank you," Abby called out as the door snapped shut. She leaned her head back into the water again. "God bless

Elda," she said, as the water sloshed over her teeth. She spit out a mouthful. "God bless Burt, and God bless Scott."

Abby smiled. Scott had saved her life. Her smile broadened. Scott had kissed her.

She felt guilty as she remembered having doubted his intentions. She felt guiltier still when she considered how far he must have carried her through the woods to safety. And his poor mother was still out there, waiting to be rescued. His poor mother and Mitch.

As her mind thawed from its cold stupor, Abby remembered. Someone had gone to a lot of trouble to keep them from ever leaving Devil's Island. Someone who had something to gain from their deaths.

Abby sat up and pulled the drain from the tub. She could have basked in the warmth of the water a lot longer, but she had work to do. Mitch and Marilyn were still alone on Devil's Island. Abby had no business relaxing until they were both safe.

After quickly drying off and pulling on the generously sized gray sweats Elda had provided, Abby opened the bathroom door to let the steam out of the room, then wiped down the mirror before throwing a dry towel over her shoulders and starting in combing through her long brown hair. Usually it wasn't too much trouble to comb through it, but she didn't have any conditioner or detangling spray, and the wind had whipped it into knots long before she'd started her bath. She sighed and got to work.

She was three-quarters of the way finished when Scott came down the hall and paused in the open doorway. He wore a navy blue sweat suit that hung too wide around his middle and too short at the wrists and ankles, though she noticed he still managed to look pretty good in it. Her heart began to beat faster, and she felt shy as she remembered his kiss. Then she caught sight of his head without his ball cap, and smiled.

"What?" he asked, touching his fingers to his forehead, which was an inch or two higher than it had been in college. He made a face. "Just think—it doesn't take me very long at all to comb through my hair."

She shook her head. "I like it. It makes you look distinguished."

"It makes me look old."

"I like it," Abby repeated.

Scott leaned one shoulder against the door frame. If Abby hadn't been watching him so closely, she might not have noticed the wince he tried to suppress.

"You're sore."

"I'm old," he said, chuckling.

"You're not old," she protested, fighting a knot in her hair. "What birthday did you just celebrate? Thirty-one?"

"Thirty-two."

"You're not old. You carried the canoe, paddled all the way here in rough weather, and then carried me. You have every right to be sore."

Scott rolled his eyes.

"And by the way—" Abby kept her eyes on the mirror, but spoke to his reflection "—thank you. You saved my life."

"You saved mine," he countered.

Unsure whether she believed him, Abby kept her eyes on the mirror and kept combing. She'd have thought after all they'd been through that she'd have gotten over her schoolgirl crush on him, but instead it seemed to have gotten worse.

Scott reached for the towel she'd left draped over the edge

of the tub. "Elda said she'd throw our clothes and towels in the wash. Burt's been in touch with the Coast Guard, but the weather's not cooperating. We can probably have our clothes washed and dried before we're ready to leave."

"Perfect." Abby ran the comb through her hair one final time, checking for any stray tangles. "I've never appreciated dry clothes so much before."

"Want me to take your things down to her?" Scott asked, pointing to Abby's jeans, which hung dripping from the towel rod over the tub.

"No, that's fine, I'm about ready." Abby patted her damp hair with the towel from her shoulders. "I can take this one, too." She reached past Scott for her jeans and gave them a tug. As they flew free of the bar, something hit the floor and skittered under the sink.

"Oops, you lost something." Scott reached for it.

"It's probably one of your mom's earrings. I can get it." Abby reached into the rear pocket of her jeans and pulled out the two earrings which had been securely nestled there. She felt her cheeks go red as she realized what had fallen out, and hoped Scott wouldn't find it.

But Scott called out from under the sink. "I've got it." He stood. "It's not an earring, but it is jewelry." He handed the diamond ring back to her, and she watched with a sinking stomach as his cheeks colored to match her own. He didn't ask her about it or comment any further. "I'll meet you downstairs," he said simply, and retreated.

Abby watched him go, furious with herself for being so careless with the ring. What if she'd lost it? She wasn't sure what bothered her more—wondering what Scott must think, or the threat of what Trevor would do if the ring didn't make it back to him.

* * *

Scott hurried down the stairs to the living room where a warm woodstove burned a cheery fire, keeping the cold and the darkness at bay. He pulled a wooden chair as close to the stove as he dared, soaking up as much warmth as he could stand after the terrific cold of the woods and the lake. But even as he stared through the stove's window at the dancing flames, Scott felt the cold and the darkness pressing in on his heart.

So, Abby had a diamond engagement ring in her pocket. He was curious about that, but it wasn't any of his business. They'd been schoolmates years and years before, and he hadn't seen her since until that morning. He had no claim on her life. But obviously someone else did, or recently had.

He needed to back away, to keep himself from becoming any more attached to her than he already felt. That kiss in the woods was a mistake, a desperate move in a moment of panic, and he wondered if she would remember it, though he doubted he'd ever forget. Abby Caldwell had always appealed to him.

He heard her feet on the steps, heard her talking with Elda in the kitchen as she handed over her wet clothes for the laundry and offered to help the older couple in any way. They turned her down, of course, and then he heard her soft footfalls on the creaky old floor as she made her way down the hall toward him. Her steps sounded tentative, almost reluctant. Or maybe he was just reading too much into things.

"Come on in, the fire's warm."

"I'm sure it feels great." At his invitation she stepped quickly past him and held her hands out to the stove. "I was beginning to wonder if I'd ever feel warm again."

"Me, too." Scott cleared his throat. Should he ask her

about the ring? No, it wasn't any of his business. But she knew he'd seen it—surely she'd be wondering what he was thinking. Perhaps it would be best if he acknowledged it and moved past it. Before he could make up his mind, Abby pulled a chair over near him, sat down and spoke.

"Remember how we were talking about who might have a motive for stranding us on the island?"

It took Scott's still-groggy mind a moment to switch topics. "Yes."

"Well, I was thinking, and I might be totally off base here," she qualified, "but you know what you said about your family's land being potentially worth a lot of money?"

Scott wanted to caution her, to assure her the whole idea was a long shot, but whether it was his exhaustion over their earlier ordeal or a still-small voice telling him to listen, he said nothing and watched her face intently as she spoke.

"It occurred to me, inheritance laws being what they are, who would get the land if you and your mother died?"

"That depends." Scott thought about it. "If Mom died, I'd inherit the land from her, and then if I died, I have two distant cousins on her side who would probably inherit it from me, although Mitch might stake some sort of claim. I don't know."

"What if you died first, or if you both died at the same time?"

Scott opened his mouth to speak, then stopped. Was she implying…

"Sorry, I'm sure it's none of my business." She rose from her chair.

Reaching up, Scott touched her arm and she sat back down. "Mitch would get it," he told her, looking into her eyes. "Mitch would get everything."

Her eyes widened at his words. "Do you think—" she started.

"Do I think what?" Fears, ideas, a jumbled mass of theories and suspicions came crashing down inside his head as though Abby had pulled open the door of an overstuffed closet and let loose more skeletons than he'd ever known were hiding there. "Do I think Mitch would stoop to murder if he thought he could get away with it? Maybe. Do I think he's bright enough to have planned something like this, or brave enough to pull it off? Not really." Scott leaned back in his chair and put his hands to his temples. He was getting a headache from all the wind and cold he'd endured.

Then he leaned forward and looked at Abby, whose sapphire-blue eyes watched him warily. "Look, I don't like my stepfather. I've never liked him. Partly that's my own bias, because I loved my father and felt my mother had betrayed his memory by marrying Mitch. But whether my dislike of the man translates into him being capable of plotting a double murder..." He shook his head.

"I'm sorry," Abby apologized. "I didn't want to suggest it, but with your mother alone on the island with him right now, and with the power cut and the radio tampered with, I guess I got spooked." Her small hand reached for his, her delicate fingers curving over his knuckles.

Scott looked down at her hand. It would have been the most natural thing in the world to take her hand, to hold her as he had in the woods. But until he knew why she was carrying an engagement ring around in her pocket, he figured he should keep his distance. He pulled his hand away.

An injured expression flashed across Abby's features. "I'm sorry," she apologized again.

Guilt immediately replaced caution, and Scott returned

her apology. "No, you're okay, I just—" He stopped, unsure what to say, whether to bring up the ring or not.

"It's okay. I get it." She leaned away from him and turned her face to the fire. Words slipped from her lips on a whisper. "You're the strong guy who helps everyone else. You don't need any support from me."

The moment she heard the words escape from her mouth, Abby felt horrible for speaking out of place. But it hurt her to see the way Scott took everything upon himself—his mother's fragility, the weight of the canoe, even her weight, as he'd carried her through the woods. She remembered an article she'd read in the college paper after the football team's sole loss his senior year. He'd blamed himself entirely for the team's loss. She didn't know him terribly well, but she could see the pattern in his life. He was a counselor by profession. He helped others all the time. But she wondered if he knew how to ask for help.

The way his lower jaw clenched, she was certain her words had upset him. But rather than raise his voice or lash out at her, he asked, "What do you mean?"

Abby wondered how she could begin to explain. It wasn't a formal thought she'd had, just a sense of Scott taking on too much and shouldering everyone else's burdens. "You've been tiptoeing around your mother all day, afraid the truth is going to break her. You can't stand your stepdad but you won't talk to her about that either."

"Abby," Scott said patiently, "I have a Ph.D. in psychology. I can deal with less than optimum interpersonal relationships, but my mother isn't equipped with that kind of objectivity. It's my duty as her son to support her."

"That's great, Scott, but who supports you?" As she

spoke, she met Scott's eyes and held his gaze. For a moment she felt as though she'd seen straight into the depths of his hurt and loss to the boy who'd lost his dad and was afraid of losing his mother, too.

Then Scott's jaw tightened and he looked away.

Abby pinched her eyes shut. She'd said too much. She didn't know Scott and didn't have any right to question him, but she felt as though she did. Though their circumstances didn't warrant it, emotionally she felt very close to him, and it hurt her to see the distance he'd put between himself and his mother. "I'm sorry. It isn't any of my business." She tucked her fingers into the warmth of her knees.

Beside her, Scott's chest rose and fell with several long, slow breaths. She could almost feel him wrestling with her words, and she wondered if he wouldn't be more comfortable if she left him alone. Just as she was about to stand, he spoke.

"I have God, Abby. I have God to support me. He is my strength and my shield."

She met his eyes again and saw the strength of his relationship with God resonating in his features. "I'm glad." She managed a sincere smile. "I'd hate for you to be alone."

Peace returned to his countenance, and they sat in silence in front of the fire.

Guilt continued to nag Abby. She wondered if her verbal attack on Scott hadn't been in part fueled by her own fear over the day's events. Ever since Trevor had appeared in her driveway the night before she'd felt as though she'd been running for her life. And while it didn't make any sense at all—couldn't make any sense, since Trevor couldn't possibly have any knowledge of what she'd done with the ring—she wondered if their situation might somehow be linked to the ring she carried in her pocket.

After several long minutes Scott spoke again. "I don't know how conscious you were earlier in the woods," he started slowly.

Immediately unsure of herself, Abby wondered if she'd said or done something embarrassing while she'd been in hypothermic shock. She hadn't confessed to having a crush on him, had she?

Scott continued, "I don't even know how conscious I was, really. I know I wasn't thinking quite straight—the cold was getting to me, and I was afraid your body temperature was dropping too low."

Realizing what he was getting at, Abby asked softly, "Is that why you kissed me?"

His eyes widened. "You remember?"

"It's not the sort of thing I'd easily forget." Abby could feel her cheeks burning. "Do you regret it?"

Scott's eyes met hers with a look she couldn't read. She could sense the importance of the answer he was about to give her, but before he so much as opened his mouth to speak, Elda poked her head into the doorway.

"Good news! Burt's just heard from the Coast Guard. They've rescued your stepdad."

Scott and Abby rose together.

"And my mother?" Scott clarified.

Elda's face fell, and she shook her head. "I'm sorry. They're still looking for her."

FIVE

Scott wanted to throw his head back and scream. Instead he stepped past Elda to the kitchen, where Burt was flipping pancakes at the stove.

"We're getting some supper for you here," Burt announced as Scott entered. "The Coast Guard guys didn't know when they'd be able to come by and get you, what with the weather and all. But we'll put some food in you and see what we can do."

"Thank you. I appreciate that." It was all Scott could do to remember his manners. "Please, Burt, did they say anything about my mother? What did Mitch have to say when she wasn't with him? Where do they think she is?"

Scott felt Abby step into the room behind him and was grateful for the gentle touch of her hand on his shoulder. He focused on relaxing his tense muscles.

Burt stepped over to the table with two plates of pancakes. "Go ahead and sit down. I'll tell you what I know."

Scott fidgeted in his seat while Burt served up the pancakes and warm Bayfield apple butter. In spite of his ravenous appetite, he didn't think he could eat until he heard more about what was going on with his mother. Still, as the scent of cinnamon and apples rose to his nose, he instinctively took a bite. It tasted delicious, but it didn't do a thing to calm his anxiety.

Burt sat opposite the two of them at the heavy round oak table, a cup of steaming coffee between his hands. "I don't know much," he began. "The Coast Guard said they'd picked up Mitchell Adams. According to Mitch, your mom had headed inland for shelter from the storm. Mitch didn't want to leave the dock, so he let her go off by herself. She might be up at the keeper's quarters or in any of the buildings, who knows? They haven't managed to get in much searching yet, but they said they'd let me know as soon as they find her. They're not too worried about finding her, but with the weather and all, they've declared it a Search and Rescue and they're bringing out more men on a couple of helicopters. Once they find her, they'll probably swing by and pick you up. In the meantime, you two can hunker down here."

Burt's update made it sound as though his mom was probably fine—and arguably more sensible than Mitch. Still, Scott had trouble accepting the positive prognosis.

"Do we need to head over there to help them? I know my mother as well as anyone. I might be able to figure out where she'd be, and Abby knows the island pretty well. We should be over there helping." Scott felt Abby's hand touch his arm, a light, reassuring pat before she turned her attention back to her plate. At least she had the good sense to eat. He made himself to take another bite, though he felt as though he was simply going through the motions. He'd need his strength if the search ran long.

"If they don't find her in any of the buildings, they'll call for reinforcements. The Coast Guard doesn't mess around when people are missing out here."

Scott wanted to persist in his line of questioning, but he knew Burt had exhausted his information. Still, it bothered him to know his mother was out there, alone in the dark somewhere in this storm. What bothered him even more was the still all-too-real possibility that someone didn't want his mother to leave the island alive. But once again, Burt wouldn't be able to tell him anything to assuage those fears. Rather than push further, he thanked his host for his help and dug into his pancakes.

When he and Abby had eaten their fill, they followed their hosts to the living room, where Burt and Elda occupied the wooden chairs. "Have a seat." Burt motioned to a two-person sofa that flanked the fire. Scott had always heard such a piece referred to as a *love* seat, but he tried not to think about that as he and Abby shared the cozy couch.

Scott saw that Burt was wearing his radio receiver on his belt, so he knew the man would answer as soon as any news came in about his mother. He put his feet close to the stove, closed his eyes and prayed in his heart for his mother. She was out there somewhere, and it tore him apart not knowing if she was okay.

"So, how'd you all get stuck on the island?" Burt asked after some silence.

While Scott listened, Abby relayed the whole story from the time Sal had left them on the island until the two of them had reached the Ranger's Station. For the most part, Burt and Elda simply listened, their weathered faces etched with concern at the news the small party had been intentionally abandoned. When Abby began to theorize possible motives for Captain Sal's crime, Elda chimed in.

"I've never heard of any Captain Sal or *Helene* 'round these parts. Granted it's a big lake, and people visit these islands from all over. But for a guy to run a water taxi business out of Bayfield and me not to have ever heard of him, now that's something."

Scott sat up a little straighter at her words. "Do you think he may have come into the area just to pull a job and leave?"

"Could be," Burt reasoned. "Not many folks know this, but these islands are a pretty wild place. A lot of open space, a lot of weather issues, not a whole lot of law enforcement for all the ground they cover. And you've got to keep in mind, we're an international border. Canada's just across the water. There've been all sorts of smuggling rings run through here. Why, pirates used to hide out in the sea caves under Devil's Island until a century ago."

Scott felt Abby tense beside him. "But the sea caves are small formations, surrounded by dangerous rocks and open sea," she protested. "How would they have provided shelter to pirates? You can't even get a kayak in most of those caves without perfect weather conditions and tremendous skill."

"Well—" Elda chuckled "—who knows? People tell some tall tales around here. Could be the caves were just a cover story for what really went on."

"I don't know," Burt defended his tale. "My grandfather was part of the crew that worked to bring them to justice. He's the one who told me about them. A good Christian man, he was. He wouldn't make up lies. Saw them with his own eyes, he did."

Elda patted his knee. "That was over a hundred years ago, Burt. It's hardly something going to help us tonight." She rose. "And speaking of, it's eight o'clock, and getting on toward our bedtime. I've made up cots in the spare rooms upstairs for you two. You can take your pick when you're ready, but I'll warn you, it gets a little chilly up there. You're welcome to spend as much time as you like down here by the fire. Plenty of wood there." She nodded toward the rack of split logs in the corner. "Good night."

Burt followed her up the stairs after promising to let them know the minute he heard any news about Marilyn. Scott couldn't ask any more of them. "Good night, and thank you."

Now alone with Abby, he thought about moving to one of the wooden chairs, but the little love seat felt cozy, and he didn't feel like forcing his tired body to move. Abby's account of their adventures had provided some distraction from his worrisome thoughts, but now that she sat silently next to him, his concerns for his mother resurfaced. Rather than stew helplessly, he decided to ask Abby the question that had been haunting him all evening.

"So, I've told you all my sorry family history," he began, turning to face her. "But I don't even know why you came out to Devil's Island this morning. Why are you here?"

Abby's eyes darted around the room as though looking for escape. He'd seen his counseling clients wear the same look when he'd asked them questions that got to the heart of their issues, so he knew he was on to something with Abby. Her reaction fed his suspicion that she was hiding something. "I used to work there years ago," she said with practiced nonchalance, as though that explained everything.

"But why now? Why today, with the tourist season basically over and the weather uncertain? It wasn't just a whim, was it?" He kept his tone noncommittal, but watched her face carefully. If his past could hold clues to their situation, perhaps hers could as well.

"I—" she started.

Abby was going to say she didn't want to talk about it.

Scott had worked with enough people in denial of their issues to know not to let her get those words out of her mouth. He cut her off. "What were you doing on Devil's Island with a diamond ring in your pocket?"

She fell silent, her face red, and she looked at her hands. There had been a time when such a response would have made him feel guilty for asking, and he'd have backpedaled to let her save face. But he'd made too many breakthroughs by pushing his clients past their areas of discomfort. And in Abby's case, whatever was bothering her might be a clue to what had happened on the island. It might even help him find his mother. He wasn't going to let her clam up just because she felt embarrassed. Besides, she'd already pushed him on his issues, so he figured it was only fair. "Is it an engagement ring?"

She met his eyes just long enough to nod.

"Yours?"

"Yes."

"Are you engaged, Abby?" Though he prided himself on keeping his emotional distance, now he felt the color creeping up his neck. He'd kissed her in the woods, however briefly. He'd feel terrible if she'd had a fiancé the whole time.

But her quick answer reassured him. "No. Not anymore, not in over five years. And I can assure you it was a mistake to begin with."

"Then why are you still carrying the ring?"

Abby didn't protest his right to ask. Perhaps she felt his questions were only fair after the way she'd challenged him on his relationship with his mother and stepfather. "I didn't. I haven't." She looked him full in the face with eyes that seemed to be searching for understanding. "The ring has been buried on Devil's Island for the past five years."

"Why?"

"My ex-fiancé and I had a rocky relationship. I'd tried breaking up with him before, but never stuck to it. I buried the ring on the island to keep myself from going back to him—that way I'd have the whole trip back to the island to come to my senses."

Scott's brow crinkled. "So why go back to get it now?"

Abby looked down at her hands. When she looked back up at him, fear haunted her eyes. "My ex-fiancé is back in town. Lately I've felt as though someone was watching me. I don't know how to explain it, just a funny sensation. I never saw anyone. But then last night, he showed up outside my house when I came home. He'd been waiting for me. He told me to give him the ring back, or else."

"Or else what?" Scott watched her intently as she spoke. A part of him found her story incredible. It didn't stand to reason that a guy who'd walked away half a decade before would suddenly come back for a small piece of jewelry. Scott wasn't sure how valuable the ring might be; in the short time he'd held it, he'd noticed the gem was large and brilliant, but given the abundance of jewelry his mother wore, he wasn't easily impressed by one ring.

Abby raised her left hand and held it out for his inspection. At first Scott only noticed the blisters on her palms from rowing the canoe across the lake. But when she pointed to the base of her ring finger, he realized she sported a deep purple bruise. "I don't know." Her voice trembled slightly. "He bent back my finger and told me he'd make sure I never wore a ring again. Now whether that means he was going to cut off my finger, or—" her voice caught "—or something worse, I don't know."

"Something worse?" Scott repeated. He could feel the

chill of the threat seeping into his own bones. "So if you give him back the ring, do you think he'll leave you alone after that?"

"I—I don't know." Abby's eyes widened again. "I guess I hadn't thought beyond that."

Scott closed his eyes and tried to think. So much had happened in the past ten hours. They had every reason to believe they'd been left to die on Devil's Island—and now this bizarre threat came from seemingly out of nowhere. Could the two possibly be connected? Perhaps his family's land had nothing to do with it. Abby may have been the intended target all along. "When were you planning to return the ring?"

"He said he wanted it back by tomorrow night. He didn't say where or how. I guess I figured he'd find me, just like he did last night."

Scott let out a long slow breath. This guy could be planning to get rid of Abby once he had what he wanted. Scott wasn't sure what shook him most—the idea of what her ex-fiancé might be planning, or the realization that he felt an overwhelming need to protect her. "Don't let yourself be alone with him," Scott cautioned her.

Abby's eyes widened. "Do you think he would still try to hurt me, even once I give him the ring back?"

"I don't know." Scott reached for her hand and studied the ugly purple bruise. Then he covered her hand with his protectively. "I don't know what's going on, but somebody's out to kill us, and you were just threatened last night. Once this guy has his ring, he won't need you anymore. What's to stop him—" Scott paused when he heard footsteps headed their way down the hall. They both looked to the entryway.

Burt stepped through to the front room.

Scott's concern for Abby was immediately eclipsed by thoughts of his mother's safety.

"The Coast Guard just called." Burt stood behind one of the wooden chairs and braced his hands on its sturdy back as though he needed the support. "They haven't found any sign of your mother yet. I told them about your offer to help look, and seeing as how the storm's letting up for now, they've agreed to send a whirlybird over to get you. They're wanting to take your fingerprints, too, to match to those they found on the radio. And I think they'll be asking you some questions. Elda's getting your clothes from the dryer. The Coasties should be here in a matter of minutes."

Scott stood. "Thank you." He stepped forward and shook Burt's hand. "You've been an enormous help. I appreciate all you've done."

"I just hope you find your mom." Burt turned as Elda entered the room.

"Here's your clothes, nice and dry, and still warm. Hurry now. You don't want to keep the Coast Guard waiting." Elda handed Scott a neatly folded stack. "Are you going over, too?" she asked Abby, who stood expectantly next to Scott.

Scott turned to Abby, and saw her face color once again.

"I—I thought I would," she stammered. "I thought I could be of some help. Unless you think I'll get in the way?" She looked to Scott, her expression one of vulnerability.

Scott felt touched that she wanted to help, and gladdened that she'd be willing to spend more time with him, even if it meant being out in the dark on a dangerous island. He put a hand on her shoulder. "If it wouldn't be too much trouble, I'd love to have your help. You know the island a whole lot better than I do. And I'm sure they'll need your fingerprints for the investigation, too."

The relieved smile on her face warmed his heart. "Then let's hurry and get changed."

Abby appreciated the heavy-duty rain ponchos Elda had insisted she and Scott wear. As for Burt's announcement the storm had let up, she didn't even want to imagine how harsh the weather must have been during the worst of it. As she and Scott stood waiting for the helicopter on the open hillside that served as Rocky Island's landing pad, the cold wind whipped at her hood and flung rain into her face from every direction.

As if the weather wasn't bad enough, Abby couldn't shake her uneasiness about returning to Devil's Island. Burt had made it sound as though most of the Bayfield Coast Guard team had been sent over to look for Marilyn, which meant Trevor would most likely be there. After hearing Scott's concerns about what Trevor might do once she handed over the ring, Abby could only pray God would protect her.

"Say, Abby?" Scott's face suddenly appeared in the limited line of sight provided by her hood, interrupting her thoughts. She jumped.

Scott placed a reassuring hand on her shoulder. "Sorry to startle you. I just wanted to ask before the Coast Guard people get here that you try not to suggest anything too incriminating about Mitch at this point."

"Why not?" Though it seemed like a stretch that Mitch may have been involved, she felt the Coast Guard team should know about every possibility. Clearly someone didn't want them leaving the island alive, and Mitch had both the motive and opportunity to make Marilyn disappear, though those facts alone didn't make him guilty.

"As I think about it, we really don't have any evidence against him. And with Mom missing and the Coast Guard on the case, I doubt there's anything more he could do at this point. I just don't want to accuse him yet. I may not like the man, but he is my mother's husband, and if I made an unwarranted accusation, Mom would be furious with me. My relationship with Mitch is strained enough as it is. If she knew I'd wrongly accused him of plotting her murder, I'm afraid she'd feel she had to take sides between us. I don't want it to come to that."

Abby bent her head close to catch every word in the whipping wind. "Of course," she agreed when he'd finished. "I won't say a thing unless there's immediate danger," she promised.

"I appreciate that." Scott gave her shoulder a squeeze before letting go. "Here they come." He pointed to the helicopter that had appeared out of the darkness. It looked like a fragile child's toy against the immensity of the black night sky.

Abby shivered, reminding herself of the many times she'd ridden in helicopters when she worked out on the islands. They were perfectly safe and a huge blessing when the rocks and waves made travel by boat too dangerous.

Despite the distraction the helicopter presented, Abby couldn't shake her concerns about Scott's choice to leave the Coast Guard in the dark on his suspicions about Mitch. Scott was clearly falling back into his usual pattern of trying to shield his mother from anything too distressing. She hoped in this case his judgment was correct. There was every possibility his good intentions could be a fatal mistake—for his mother, and for both of them.

As soon as the copter touched down, she and Scott

rushed forward to the opening door and were helped aboard by a smiling young Coast Guard crewmember. Abby recognized the blonde woman from seeing her around Bayfield, though she didn't know her name.

"I'm Tracie Crandall," the Coastie introduced herself and helped them get situated as the helicopter rose again and headed back to Devil's Island. "I know you've got a lot of questions, so let me tell you what we've learned so far. In an initial check of the buildings on the island, we've found no sign of Marilyn, but that doesn't rule out the possibility that we've missed her, or even overlooked a building. It's been dark and stormy the whole time we've been looking, and that complicates things.

"We were able to contact the accountant whose name you forwarded to us. He looked into her accounts and discovered the last charge to any of her credit cards was at the Seagull Bay Motel yesterday afternoon. That doesn't mean the cards haven't been used since then— the activity simply may not have been recorded yet. He's going to stay on top of it and let us know if anything comes through."

Tracie took a deep breath. "Now, about this Captain Sal," she said, watching their faces, "we can't find any record of anyone by that name, nor of any boat called the *Helene*. Are you sure that's what he went by?"

"Yes," both Abby and Scott agreed.

"Well, then I'm going to need to get a description from you once we get on the ground. Here we are now. We're going to land by the old keeper's quarters." She braced herself and the helicopter touched down.

Once on the ground, Abby hurried with the others through the spitting rain to the structure, where the lights were on, though no one appeared to be inside. Abby assumed they were all out searching.

"They've restored power," Tracie explained. "We wouldn't have known to bring the right tools if Burt hadn't passed along your message about it being cut, though, so thank you. Fixing the radio will be more difficult, but we've brought out another unit."

While Tracie took their fingerprints, Abby and Scott did their best to describe everything they remembered about Captain Sal and his boat.

"I thought from the sound of his accent he was probably local," Abby admitted. "He had that Northern Wisconsin way of pronouncing things."

"The local dialect can be a pretty tough one to fake," Tracie noted, "but it covers a pretty wide area. I've heard it as far west as North Dakota, and the Canadians have a very similar way of talking. Are you familiar with it?"

"Yes," Abby admitted. "And you're right—I didn't hear him talk enough to rule that out." She wished she'd paid more attention on the boat, but she hadn't known then it would be important.

Scott had been watching out the window while the women talked. He spoke up. "I don't know that I can recall anything more of importance, but I can tell you I'm itching to get out there and start looking. Do you mind if I poke around outside?"

"Yes, but try to stay close until I get done with Abby's prints," Tracie requested. "Then the two of you can head out as a team. We don't want anyone going too far alone. And keep an eye on the weather—this storm may well get worse again. Here's a flashlight."

Scott accepted the high-powered torch with thanks and

hurried out. Abby watched him go, then took advantage of his absence to inquire of Tracie about Mitch.

"So, Tracie, did Mitch go back to Bayfield already?"

"Yes." The other woman methodically pressed another of Abby's fingers against the sensor that would record her prints for computer analysis. "He'd been standing out in the rain and was in a hurry to get into some dry clothes. We assured him we'd let him know right away if we learned anything."

Abby nodded, cognizant of the promise she'd made to Scott about not suggesting anything incriminating about Mitch. "So where is he now?"

Tracie pressed the last of Abby's fingers to the sensor. "I suppose he headed back to his hotel. I don't know. Is it important?"

"It may be."

"Then let me find out." Tracie finished and quickly got on the radio. "The guys who escorted him to Bayfield said he was headed back to the Seagull Bay Motel," she explained.

Abby had heard as much from the transmission. "How was he going to get there? Was he driving?"

Tracie passed along the question, and the reply came back clearly.

"He drove his own vehicle."

"Are you sure?" Abby scowled, thinking quickly. Marilyn had said her keys were in her purse, which she'd left aboard the *Helene*. They'd assumed Captain Sal would steal the vehicle. But if Captain Sal hadn't stolen it, then why had he abandoned them on the island? Abby stepped closer to Tracie. "Can you ask them if they noticed what kind of vehicle?"

Tracie nodded and forwarded the question.

Once again, the answer transmitted clearly. "A red Escalade, the latest model."

SIX

"I need to go find Scott," Abby told Tracie, excusing herself quickly and heading toward the back door.

"Take a flashlight," Tracie reminded her.

"Thanks," Abby said, her mind mostly on getting to Scott and letting him know what she'd found out. Part of her wanted to tell Tracie what was up, but she doubted Scott would agree that the news warranted revealing their suspicions about Mitch. Still, it didn't add up. If Captain Sal was nothing more than a petty crook, then why wouldn't he take one of the most valuable pieces he'd managed to steal? If he'd only been in it for monetary gain, wouldn't cutting the power and radio lines buy him enough time to drive the vehicle out of the area before anyone tracked him down?

The rain had picked up while she'd been in the house, and Abby pulled her hood up, turning her whole upper body this way and that as she stood on the path and wondered which way Scott would have gone. He'd promised Tracie he wouldn't go far. She headed down the path, trying to think of where Marilyn might have gone, which would then translate into where Scott would have headed out looking for her.

The underbrush was tangled and thick beyond the small yard behind the house. Abby couldn't imagine Scott heading out through the dense growth, much less Marilyn. But as she flashed her light into the woods to the left of the path, she saw the movement of a large, looming figure.

"Scott?" she called out. The wind whipped her words away. The shape looked human, but Abby realized in the deceptive darkness she might be mistakenly trying to communicate with a bear.

The figure advanced closer. He had Scott's height and broad build—it wasn't a bear, anyway. Abby stepped farther down the path toward him. "Scott?" She squinted into the rain, trying to decide. Between the darkness and everything else going on, her nerves were a little on edge. The figure came closer, though his gait didn't seem like Scott's, and he looked to be more widely built. Still, there was something familiar about him.

The mysterious figure stepped toward her, and Abby felt a cold jolt of fear as she recognized him.

"Hey, Abby." Trevor's words were casual, but his tone held a menacing bite.

"Trevor." Abby would have preferred to meet a bear. She tried to look behind her, wondering how far she'd gone from the house. Her hood blocked her view. She decided to act casual while she began to inch backward. "What are you doing out here?"

"Search and Rescue," her former fiancé said, drawing himself even taller until he loomed over her, and puffing out the Coast Guard symbol on his parka.

Abby recalled that Trevor was part of the Coast Guard, though for a long time he'd been stationed far from Bayfield. Apparently he was now part of the local team.

"Find anything?" Abby asked, carefully backing down the path. She didn't want to draw attention to her retreat, but she was mindful of Scott's warning not to allow herself to be alone with Trevor. His caution made sense—especially now when she was in Trevor's threatening presence. Once she gave Trevor the ring, she'd be of no more use to him. Would he leave her alone then—or choose to get rid of her for good?

"Not yet. Not much here to find. What about you? Did you find that diamond ring I gave you?" His heavy eyebrows shaded his eyes, cloaking them in blackness.

Abby looked behind her. It was still a good hundred feet to the house. She slid her hand under her parka, reaching for the ring. She wondered if she dared hand it to him and then attempt to run away. Would she have time? "Trevor, there's a woman missing and this storm seems to be getting worse. It's hardly the time to be concerned about an old piece of jewelry." Her fingers dug against the thick fabric, which had shrunken slightly when Edna had baked her pants in the dryer, making it that much more difficult for her to reach the ring.

"Proper etiquette says that if an engagement doesn't work out, the woman should return the ring." Trevor stepped closer to her.

"Proper etiquette?" Abby repeated incredulously, as the tip of one numb finger brushed against the ring, pushing it farther into her pocket. She took another step backward and tried to reach deeper for the ring. Her mind spun as she tried to keep Trevor at bay with words. "What does etiquette have to say about a guy who cheats on his fiancée? Does he still get his ring back? What if he cheats twice?" Abby had never nailed down just how unfaithful Trevor had been. By the time she'd heard the rumors, he'd apparently

determined himself to be exempt from the restraints of faithfulness.

Her words clearly irritated the large Coast Guardsman. "Abby, you'd better find the ring. I don't have time for your petty jealousy." He moved closer, close enough he could reach out and grab her if he tried. She didn't want to think what he might do if he got hold of her.

"*My* petty jealousy?" Abby tried to inch backward, but between her hood and the darkness, she couldn't see anything behind her. "You're the one who's drudging up ancient history in the middle of a Search and Rescue. In case you've forgotten, Marilyn Adams is lost. Her life may be in danger, and every minute counts in our search. And you want to stand around and yak about some old piece of jewelry?" She couldn't reach the ring. It had disappeared past a crease in the stiff denim, and she could have sobbed with fear and frustration.

"Testy, testy," Trevor clucked, shaking his head in a pitying fashion as he continued to move toward her. "Abby, you've really got to learn to control your temper if you're ever going to find a guy willing to put up with you. Most men aren't interested in your unstable little dramas." He stepped forward again. "Most guys don't like being manipulated into proposing."

He was close, far too close, and Abby recognized the expression on his face. It *almost* looked concerned. It almost appeared caring, but it was everything but. When it came to manipulation, Trevor was a master. It had taken Abby far too long to realize he couldn't be trusted. She had to get away from him. Though she couldn't see anything behind her, she stepped backward in faith—and slammed into something hard.

An arm came around her, pulling her back, pulling her tight against a muscular chest.

Abby's heart stood still.

"Is there a problem?" Scott's voice met her ears.

Abby sagged ever-so-slightly against him. She was so relieved to have him there, but at the same time, she realized he must have heard all the nasty things Trevor had said about her. Her heart sank. How could she even begin to explain away Trevor's accusations?

"No problem, unless you consider Abby's refusal to cooperate with the Search and Rescue to be a problem."

Abby's spine stiffened. Trevor had sunk to a new low.

But Scott didn't budge, didn't question her. Instead he stared down Trevor. "Abby has already cooperated far beyond what you have any right to ask," Scott retorted, his arm pulling her more snugly against him, comforting and protective. "If your mission succeeds, it will be because of her contributions."

"Whatever." Trevor turned away. "I've got a body to find." He stomped off into the woods.

"I'm sorry," Abby apologized, cringing at Trevor's use of the word *body*. She hadn't yet allowed herself to consider the possibility that Marilyn might already be dead. "He's completely inappropriate, completely irresponsible..." Her voice faded as Scott lifted her chin gently until she looked into his eyes.

"Trevor Price has always been a total jerk," Scott stated bluntly. "I'm just sorry you had to put up with him as long as you did."

Abby clamped her eyes shut. Scott's words were comforting, but she had to tell him the whole story. "Trevor Price is my old fiancé. He's the one who gave me the ring."

"I know. That's why I'm so sorry."

At the look of pain that crossed Abby's face, Scott wished he had time to explain his own history with Trevor Price, but there wasn't time. They'd found no sign of his mother, and the weather was getting worse. "Come on, let's look this way."

"But Trevor just went that way."

"Yeah, and I don't trust him. So let's not let him get too far ahead." Scott stepped resolutely down the path.

"Wait, Scott." Abby's hold on his arm tightened. "There's something you need to know."

Sensing what she was going to say, Scott stopped her. "Abby, I know Trevor just said a lot of libelous things about you. I heard him, but I don't care about that right now. After we find my mom, you and I can sit down and straighten all that stuff out. But right now I just want to find my mother."

"It's not about that." Abby's voice wavered, and Scott sensed for the first time that evening that her patience was beginning to wear thin. "It's about Mitch. I asked Tracie where he was, and she talked to the guys who took him back to Bayfield. Scott, he drove himself back to the hotel in a red Escalade—the latest model. Doesn't that match the description of your mother's car?"

Scott blinked away the rain that kept finding its way under his hood. So Sal hadn't taken the car, then. Hadn't he gone back to Bayfield? If he had, why hadn't he taken one of the most valuable items he'd managed to steal?

A shifting flash of light in the darkness made him spin and look—just as an apparition appeared. "What was that?" he asked, taking a tentative step closer to where he'd seen the movement.

"Blowhole." Abby raised her voice to be heard over the storm. "When the water gets rough like this, the waves hit the sea caves hard enough they actually blow spray up through fissures in the rocks. Watch. You'll probably see another one."

Sure enough, as the two stood looking, another blast of white appeared where Scott had seen the first one. He shuddered. "That's creepy," he shouted against the wind.

"I know. I think that's why the Chippewa called this place Evil Spirit Island—because the blowholes look like evil spirits dancing in the storm." As Abby spoke, Scott had to lean close to her face to hear, or else the wind would have whipped her words away.

"That's where the name Devil's Island comes from?" Scott clarified.

"Exactly. Sounds innocent enough, doesn't it? Although I've still never liked the place. There's just something about it…something evil." They'd stopped moving again, the furious storm hampering their progress.

Scott huddled so close to Abby their hoods formed an intimate protected space. "Well, if Burt's story about pirates is true, I'm sure plenty of ungodly activities occurred in this place."

"It's hard to imagine anyone getting a decent-size boat in under this island. I've been through some of the caves in a kayak. They're natural formations, never intended to be navigated by boat. How the pirates could have used them as shelter, I can't imagine." Abby's breath felt warm on his chin, and Scott could just make out the faint scent of cinnamon and apples on her breath.

"Burt seemed pretty confident the old stories were true," Scott reminded her, his own imagination sparked by the possibilities and the presence of the blowholes. "What if there was a hollow space under the island? Or what if it wasn't even that big—just big enough for a person to hide—or fall into." He let his forehead touch Abby's temple. He told himself he was getting close to her so she could hear him, but on a certain level, he was aware of the comfort that small contact brought him. "What if my mother went inland seeking shelter, got lost in the rain and slid into a blowhole? She could be stuck in there, unable to get out, and we wouldn't know it until we got close enough to hear her cries for help."

"In this wind, you wouldn't hear her cries unless you were almost on top of her."

"So it's a possibility, isn't it? We need to consider all the possibilities."

"True." Abby sounded reluctant to accept his theory. A furious gust of wind hit them, pelting them with even heavier rain. "Maybe somebody knows more about where the blowholes are located. But for now, we should get back to the keeper's quarters. This storm is getting worse."

Scott cast one last look around the dark woods. He had no idea where Trevor had slunk off to. "I suppose you're right. Let's head back."

Tracie waved them over as soon as they stepped into the house. "You two need to get on that copter while we're still able to get you back to Bayfield. This storm is beginning to look ugly. Most of us are heading in."

Scott wanted to protest, to insist on staying to look for his mother, but he knew visibility was next to nothing, making the island a dangerous place for all of them, especially if the storm was getting worse. Reluctantly, he acknowledged the best thing they could do for his mom at this point was get a decent night's sleep and try again in the morning. Still, he felt his heart break as the copter lifted off the ground. He gripped Abby's un-injured hand tightly while he prayed silently for his mother's safety.

Scott checked his watch. It was just after ten o'clock. There had been a time during his college days when staying out much later on a Saturday wouldn't have fazed him. Now he felt his exhaustion to his bones, as well as a nagging headache from the wind. But much as his body wanted to turn in for the night, in his heart he knew he needed to find Mitch and sort things out. It bothered him that Mitch hadn't stuck around to help find his mother. But more than that, Scott felt troubled by the nagging pos-sibility that Mitch might have engineered their abandon-ment as part of an elaborate scheme to cover up their murder so he could inherit the family land. Though it seemed like a stretch, he had to consider the possibility.

He turned to Abby, but noticed she was already nodding off. She needed her sleep. He kept silent until they landed at the Coast Guard station in Bayfield, then nudged her awake and draped a supportive arm around her shoulders as they made their way to their cars.

It was only a couple of blocks from the Coast Guard landing pad to the parking lot nearest the pier. Streetlights illuminated an upscale neighborhood of lakeside condo-miniums and tidy landscaping. Though the wind blew hard and the rain continued to spit, the weather was much tamer on the mainland, insulated by the buffer of the islands, than it had been twenty miles out to sea on Devil's Island.

They reached her car first. "So, what's your plan?" she asked as she unlocked her door.

"I thought I might head down to the Seagull Bay and see what Mitch is up to."

"Mind if I come with you?"

"I was kind of hoping you'd offer."

"Hop in. I'll drive."

There was no sign of an Escalade in the motel parking lot. "Stop at the office," Scott suggested. "It's possible he's checked out." He didn't want to think what that would mean. If Mitch left town while his mother was still missing, Scott would no longer be able to disregard him as a suspect.

Abby pulled her car to a stop and accompanied Scott into the small office where an older couple sat in easy chairs in front of a small television. The woman worked on a needlework project on her lap. They both looked up when Scott and Abby entered.

"You folks need a room?" the man asked.

"Actually, I'm looking for my stepdad, Mitchell Adams. He and my mother were staying at your motel and I'd like to get in touch with him, but I don't see their vehicle."

"To my knowledge they haven't checked out." The man looked to his wife.

The older woman spoke up. "No, but I think I saw him drive past ten minutes ago or so. Don't they drive one of those big fancy SUVs?"

"Yes," Scott confirmed.

"That's right," the woman affirmed, turning her attention back to her needlework. "Saw him drive by not ten minutes ago. Don't know which way he headed, but he's paid up for the night and still has his key, so I expect he'll be back. Care to leave a message?"

"No, thank you, that won't be necessary." Scott waved and followed Abby back into the night. "Well," he began once they were in her car, "you're the local expert. Mitch comes back from the island, he's hungry, where would he go? What's open at this hour?"

"Not much." Abby drove back to the parking lot where they'd left his car. "A couple of restaurants maybe, but now that the tourist season is over, it gets to be slim pickings, even on the weekends. Bayfield only has about six hundred residents in the off-season. He might have headed down the road to Washburn. It's a bigger town—there'd be more open at this hour. Want to split up and look for him?"

"Sounds like a plan," Scott agreed. "Since you know the town, you can check out the local hangouts. I'll head down the highway and see if I can catch up to him. Let's make sure we have each other's phone numbers so we can stay in touch." He pointed to his car in the parking lot, and Abby came to a stop in the empty parking space beside it.

They put each other's cell numbers on speed dial, and then Scott reached for her hand. "Before we go, let's pray. I think we could use some guidance."

Abby kept her eyes closed tight while Scott prayed. She felt convinced the next step was to find Mitch. Whether he was somehow behind Marilyn's disappearance or simply a witness to it, he'd have information that could help them. She silently gave her concerns to God while Scott spoke reassuring words.

Scott closed the prayer with an emphatic *amen* and headed to his car. "Call me if you learn anything," he insisted.

"You, too," she called back, then pulled quickly away. There weren't many places Mitch was likely to be, but it would take a while to check them all. She didn't want to waste any more time.

Abby turned out of the parking lot onto Rittenhouse Avenue. One block later, she spotted a huge red SUV in the parking lot of Greunke's, the tavern that had been a landmark in Bayfield for longer than the port had been a town. Thanking God for his provision, Abby pulled into the parking lot and left her car in the shadow of the Escalade.

For a fleeting moment she thought about calling Scott. But no, she'd already seen how poorly Mitch and Scott communicated with one another. Scott would raise Mitch's hackles before they'd have a chance to learn anything. She hoped to get on his good side. If that failed to yield any information, she could always call Scott later.

Abby entered the restaurant quietly. Given the late hour and the off-season, the usually packed restaurant appeared to be empty. Abby crept in as stealthily as she dared, approaching the first empty table before the long lunch counter that ran the length of the main room. Off to her right, smaller dining rooms branched off, their doorways just beyond her. She recognized the waitress, a woman named Deb, who was stacking malt glasses just behind the lunch counter. When Deb looked up from her glasses, Abby made eye contact with her and motioned for the waitress to join her.

Deb nonchalantly left her malt glasses and met Abby by the entryway. Abby held one finger to her lips as the woman approached. "I'm looking for the man whose SUV is parked out front," Abby whispered once the waitress was close enough to hear. "But I don't want him to see me."

Deb smiled and blew a bubble with her gum. When it popped, she said quietly, "He's in the far dining room, but he's facing this way. If you go in there, he'll see you."

"Mind if I sit in that booth?" Abby pointed to the spot just before the wide doorway of the far dining room.

"No problem. You want to order something?"

After a day of fasting on Devil's Island, Abby's stomach grumbled at the thought of food, but since she didn't know what her plans were, she reluctantly shook her head. "I'll still leave you a tip, though."

"Don't worry about it," Deb replied, then went back to the malt glasses.

With a deep breath and another internal prayer for guidance, Abby settled into the booth and considered how best to approach Mitch. Shifting her weight as she sat on the bench, Abby felt a prickle from the earrings in her back pocket. Perhaps that would be her excuse for talking to him—she could approach him on the pretext of returning Marilyn's earrings. From there, perhaps they could strike up a conversation. She saw Deb disappear into the kitchen.

Now was her chance to speak to him privately. Abby stood, ready to exit her booth and approach Mitch, when she heard him speak.

"Yeah, it's Mitch. Where are you guys?"

There was a pause, and Abby's heart began to beat rapidly. Was he on the phone talking to Scott?

"Yeah, well, wait for my signal and take her back out to the island. I cut the brake line on the kid's car. The slick roads and the bluffs should take care of the rest. No!"

Abby jumped at the sound of Mitch pounding his fist against the table.

"Not until I call you," Mitch insisted angrily. "I have to make sure he's dead before you knock her off. *He has to die first.*"

Much as she wanted to stay and hear the rest of Mitch's conversation, Abby realized Scott's life was in imminent danger. If Mitch had tampered with his brakes, then the winding road to Washburn was a death sentence. Abby had to get in touch with him immediately.

She leaped from the booth and headed toward the door, simultaneously pulling her cell phone from her purse as she went. In her haste, she knocked into a chair and it crashed to the floor. The last thing she heard before she dived out the door was Mitch's loud voice carrying through the empty restaurant. "Wait a second, what was that?"

Abby ran to her car, starting the ignition and pulling on her seat belt while she hit the speed dial for Scott's phone. As she pulled onto the road, she saw the rear backup lights illuminate on the Escalade. So he'd seen her.

"Hello?" Scott's voice answered a moment later.

"Scott? Oh, thank God. How are your brakes?" Though Abby normally refused to talk on her phone while driving, under the circumstances, she considered *not* talking to be the more dangerous option.

"Now that you mention it, they felt a little soft earlier." Scott paused. "They're gone. My brakes are gone."

"Where are you?"

"I just passed Port Superior."

Abby could place the spot easily on her mental map of Highway Thirteen. For the next several miles, the highway was lined on either side by steep bluffs: to the right, sheer cliffs jutted upward in alternating steep slopes and sharp walls of brownstone; to the left, the land dropped off precipitously to the rocky shores of Lake Superior. She sucked in a worried breath but kept her voice calm. "Try to slow down. Whatever you do, don't accelerate, and look for a spot to turn off if you can. I'm coming up behind you, but you've got a good lead on me. Are you still okay?"

"I'm fine," Scott assured her. "But my parking brake isn't working, either."

"Yeah, Mitch probably took care of that, too."

"Mitch?"

"Yes. I'll explain later." The bright flash of headlights in her rearview mirror told Abby that Mitch was still behind her—and closing in. "You just keep your car on the road. I'm going to call 911. Bye."

Abby didn't have time to wait for Scott's goodbye. Instead, she ended the call and then, accelerating to stay ahead of Mitch as they left the town of Bayfield behind, she dialed the number for emergency assistance, quickly relaying her position and Scott's before explaining, "My friend's brakes have been tampered with, and the guy who did it is tailgating me."

"One moment, please." After a pause, the voice that had answered spoke again. "I don't have an officer in the immediate area. Could you give me a description of your vehicles?"

Abby answered several questions, while at the same time continuing to accelerate to stay ahead of Mitch. The road began to wind around trees and bluffs, its smooth black surface slick from the spitting rain that was starting to crystallize and hit her windshield in filmy chunks of sleet, fogging over the inside. Mitch was so close now, his headlights lit up the interior of her car, making it even more difficult for her to see out.

"Sorry," she said finally, cutting off the dispatcher mid-question. "I have to go. Please get somebody out here as soon as you can!" She closed the call and dropped the phone onto her lap before cranking up her defrost and pressing her foot down harder on the gas pedal. She had to get away from Mitch or she would lead him right to

Scott. Worse yet, if Scott was going slowly enough on the road, she could end up ramming him and then being rammed by Mitch. She had to find out where Scott was— he was bound to be close. She picked up the phone and hit his speed dial again, then waited for him to answer. One ring. Two. Three. Four. Five.

SEVEN

Scott eyed the steep driveway as his car approached at a forty-mile-per-hour roll. The sound of the ringing phone barely penetrated his thoughts as his fingers tightened around the steering wheel. Could he take it? The drive was narrow and lined with brownstone boulders on the steep downhill side. With a quick prayer, he turned off the highway and felt his tires scramble to hold on the wet gravel.

The car eased up the hill, slowing steadily. Scott hoped he'd be able to shove the car into Park once it reached its nadir of speed. If not, once the car exhausted its forward momentum, he'd likely start sliding backward again. And once he slid backward, there was nowhere to go but back onto the slick highway—backward. He'd be in a more dangerous spot than before.

The ringing phone pierced his thoughts and he grabbed it. "Abby?"

"Yes. Where are you?"

"On a driveway, about half a mile past that old abandoned house."

"I just passed the house. I should be coming up on you shortly."

"Good. I want you to drive up behind me and keep my car from rolling backward. Can you do that?"

Silence. Scott felt like kicking himself for trusting Mitch as much as he had. If the man was out to kill him, of course he'd resort to more desperate measures once his initial plan failed. And once again, he'd managed to get Abby caught between them. If something happened to her because of him, he didn't know how he'd ever forgive himself.

"I—I think so." Abby sounded scared. "Mitch is right behind me. We're going really fast."

Scott's car crept to a crawl. He tried the parking brake again, but there was nothing there; no response when he pushed the brake to the floor, either.

"I see you!" Abby gasped into the phone. "Here I come!"

Scott looked in his mirror and saw Abby's car hurtle off the highway. "Don't hit your brakes until you've got traction!" he shouted into the phone, hoping she could still hear him.

Sure enough, her car fishtailed crazily before he saw the red of her brake lights reflected in the steam and spray they'd thrown up. Just beyond her, his mother's red SUV streaked by before slamming on its brakes. Mitch apparently hadn't expected her to turn off. The truck wheeled around and tore up the driveway, but Mitch's miscalculation bought them time.

Abby's brakes squealed as her car careened up the narrow road. Scott braced himself, preparing to escape by opening his door and unlatching his seat belt as his own car reached its zenith and began its backward descent. In another second, he lurched forward at the rough kiss of their bumpers and saw the fear on Abby's face through the windshield.

Mitch was less than twenty yards away. Throwing himself out his open door, Scott ran toward Abby as she leaped from her own car. Just before the Escalade slammed into Abby's car, Scott grabbed her by her shoulders and tugged her over the brownstone ledge into the leaves and underbrush of the sparse woods that tapered off rapidly down the edge of the bluff. They rolled for several yards until Scott felt his back slam into a thick sapling, which shuddered slightly at the impact of their bodies.

Above them, the sounds of crunching metal and shattering glass gave way to curses and growling, incomprehensible rage as Mitch jumped from the wrecked Escalade and snapped on a flashlight. The beam swept over their heads.

"Shh," Scott whispered against Abby's ear. "Mitch is looking for us. Lie absolutely still." He held Abby tight to his chest and prayed silently. Though the falling rain and fallen leaves camouflaged their location, it would only be a matter of minutes, possibly seconds, before Mitch found them. Scott wasn't terribly worried until he heard a distinctive click, which sounded for all the world like a gun's safety being taken off.

Abby buried her face against the quilted softness of Scott's flannel shirt. She could feel his heart pumping madly beneath her check, and heard the crackle of sleet hitting leaves all around them. The earth smelled damp, pungent with fall, and she pondered momentarily the irony of her situation. Had it not been for the deranged would-be killer above them, she'd have considered her circumstances to be rather romantic.

The Lord is my shepherd, I shall not want. The Psalm sprang back into her head. She pinched her eyes tight and repeated the lines until they echoed faintly with the sound of…sirens. Drawing closer. She felt Scott's arms tense around her.

An instant later another stream of curses erupted above them, and the flashlight beam disappeared. From the scrambled noises she heard, Abby deduced that Mitchell had climbed back into the crashed Escalade and was trying to get away.

The engine roared to life above them.

"No," Abby hissed into Scott's shirt. "Please, Lord, don't let him get away." She lay motionless, still not daring to move, as she listened to the crunch of tires on gravel on the road above her. The sirens grew louder, violently loud as the emergency vehicle came up the narrow driveway. The vehicle skidded to a stop, its red and blue lights piercing the woods, and Abby could picture it blocking the road, preventing Mitch's escape.

Then she heard a flurry of crackling leaves above her a half second before a loud voice shouted, "Sheriff, freeze!"

After that, everything happened quickly. Scott jumped up and scrambled past her. She shouted at him to stay down, but he ran after the retreating figure who was half running, half sliding through the steep stand of woods that clung tenaciously to the side of the bluff. At the same time, she heard two shots fired above her, and more crunching leaves as another figure darted past. She huddled in the darkness and prayed for Scott's safety as harsh men's voices echoed off the brownstone and gave way to the sounds of their struggle.

Scott's voice. She heard Scott's voice, sounding strained and winded, but determined as he insisted, "You're not going anywhere."

Cautiously, she raised her head and peeked in the direction of Scott's voice. Headlight beams shot through the darkness at discordant angles, dancing with the lights of the sheriff's vehicle and the steam that rose from the rotting leaves to meet the sleet in the air. Then out of the darkness and fog she saw three figures step into the light. Sheriff Jacobsen and Scott, with Mitch between them.

Much as she wanted to run to Scott and throw her arms around him, grateful he was unharmed, she held back, reluctant to risk doing anything that might give Mitch an opportunity to escape. Scott and the sheriff were having a tricky enough time picking their way up the steep, slippery incline while restraining Mitch, whose wrists were shackled behind him.

Abby found her way up through the slick leaves and reached the brownstone ledge just as the sheriff shoved Mitch into the back of his patrol car and slammed the door. Scott's voice carried through the eerily still night. "I don't know. He's my stepfather. My mother is missing—the Coast Guard has been searching for her out on Devil's Island. He rammed into our cars."

Realizing Scott had no idea about the details of the conversation she'd overheard, Abby rushed forward. "Please," she addressed Sheriff Jacobsen, "can you get in touch with the Coast Guard? Mitch knows where Scott's mom is. I overheard him giving someone orders to take her back out to the island. He also said he'd cut Scott's brakes." She turned to Scott. "I came after you as soon as I found out."

Abby wanted more than anything to lean against Scott's strong shoulders again, to feel the support of his sturdy arms around her, but when she looked up through the spitting sleet into his face, she saw the tension that knit his features and realized all his attention was focused on talking to the sheriff. Once again, she had to remind herself that, though she felt close to him after the day's ordeals and from knowing him years before, they were still relative strangers. She had no right to turn to him for comfort, no matter how shaken she felt by the evening's events.

Sheriff Jacobsen listened while Scott explained, "We need more people working to find my mother. Someone obviously intends to harm her. Every minute counts." His eyes flashed from the backseat window of the sheriff's car, to Abby, then back to the sheriff again. "I don't know who I can trust anymore. Please, step up the level of this investigation."

Sheriff Jacobsen nodded. "I'll see what I can do." He got on his radio, and after some back-and-forth, explained, "A team from the Coast Guard is heading out here right now. They'll need you two to wait and come in with them for questioning. They're going to call in reinforcements to work the case. It seems they already have everyone on the Bayfield team doing everything they can to find your mother."

Abby knew the Coast Guard, with its greater resources and manpower, often operated in a law enforcement capacity on the mainland, especially when the islands were involved. The Bayfield village police force was simply too small. "Thank you." She glanced back at Scott. He was staring at the back passenger window of the sheriff's car, though the dark tint made it difficult to see inside.

Scott turned to her, his eyes stormy. "What happened? I just left you twenty minutes ago." His expression looked hard, almost accusatory.

The exhaustion she'd been ignoring hit Abby like a wave, and she wanted to crumple into a ball and cry.

Instead she tugged on Scott's sleeve, pulled him off to the side, and explained. "I saw a red Escalade parked outside of Greunke's, so I went inside. When the waitress told me where Mitch was sitting, I waited in a booth out of sight. While I was trying to sort out what to do next, I heard him on his phone. He sounded angry." Abby tried hard to recall exactly what Mitch had said, and in what order. "Whoever he was talking to, he told them to take your mom back out to the island, but to wait for his signal, because you had to die first."

"And then what?"

"That's all. When I heard him say he'd cut your brakes, I knew I had to warn you. I got up and ran out of the restaurant so fast I knocked over a chair. Mitch heard me and came after me. That's all I know." She watched Scott's face as she spoke. His brow furrowed, and she could see him struggling to come to terms with the implications of what she'd overheard. Then he turned to her and his face softened.

"I'm sorry you got caught up in this." He looked up the drive to her smashed car. "You've been through a lot on my family's account, and it hasn't been fair to you."

Abby met his eyes and saw the sincere regret there. The pit of her stomach felt guilty. *Had* all of her troubles been on account of some plot Mitch had cooked up to kill off Scott and his mother? No, her troubles had started with Trevor. Abby opened her mouth to speak, but before she could think of what to say, a Coast Guard truck pulled up.

As if on cue, Trevor Price stepped out from the driver's seat. *He* was the Coast Guard official who would be asking her questions? Abby's stomach sank even further, then gave a hopeful leap when Tracie Crandall exited the passenger side of the vehicle. Though Abby didn't know

Tracie very well, she could be certain anyone else would give her a greater benefit of the doubt than Trevor.

While Trevor spoke with Sheriff Jacobsen, Tracie approached Scott and Abby. "We're going to take you guys back to the station," she said, her expression guarded but faintly welcoming. "It's late, you've got to be tired, and we've got a lot of questions to ask." Then she grinned at them. "And we've got coffee there."

Abby beamed her appreciation. "Thank you." She looked warily over at Trevor and the sheriff. "What about…"

Tracie placed her hand on Abby's arm. "Mitchell Adams is part of our investigation now. Trevor is going to go with Sheriff Jacobsen to take him in. You two can come back to the station with me. We've called in a team to check out Scott's brakes and investigate the crash, so for right now, this driveway is a crime scene." Her eyes followed the driveway up the hill. "Fortunately, I believe the snowbirds who live at this address have gone south for the winter, so they won't mind us blocking their driveway."

Abby nodded and started back toward the truck, then remembered something very important. "The phone." She turned to face Tracie. "We need to get Mitch's cell phone. He was on the phone with the people who have Marilyn—his phone should have a record of the call."

"Of course," Tracie agreed. "We'll have a crew out here quickly, and they'll check the vehicles for anything of importance. I'll alert them to the significance of the phone. But for right now, I need you two to come back to headquarters with me so I can take your statements."

Abby repeated the one-sided conversation she'd overheard as close to verbatim as she could recall. Tracie went over her statement several times. To her understanding, Scott was in another room, giving his version of what had happened. And though she didn't know if Scott would appreciate it, Abby went ahead and explained how his family's land fit into the picture. She'd only promised to keep it a secret unless his life was in danger. In her opinion, they'd crossed that line. He might be furious with her afterward, but she'd prefer that to him ending up dead. The authorities needed to know what they were up against, or at least be aware of the possibilities.

To her relief, though her story was slightly confused and certain parts were admittedly conjecture, Tracie seemed to think her theories about Mitch were plausible. More important, the other woman understood Abby's insistence that Mitch be questioned as quickly as possible. Every moment they wasted put Marilyn's life in greater danger.

As Tracie had promised, the Coast Guard station had hot coffee. Abby sipped a little, mindful that she'd want to be able to fall asleep if she ever got the chance. With any luck, Mitch would tell them where they could find Marilyn, and they'd have her back before morning.

"The good news," Tracie concluded, after recording Abby's thorough statement, "is that it sounds as though Marilyn is still alive, and possibly being held somewhere here on the mainland. If her kidnappers are waiting for a signal from Mitch before they act, then we just need to get information on her whereabouts from him before he gives them other instructions."

Abby agreed. "I just wish I knew what Mitch was referring to when he told them to wait for his signal. He may have been talking about waiting to take her back out to the island, but I don't know. It almost sounded as though they were headed out there already, because Mitch was so insistent on making sure Scott died first. I think the signal was for them to kill Marilyn."

"In that case, we'll have to get Mitch back here in a hurry and put the pressure on him to share what he knows. Marilyn's life may be in imminent danger. I wonder if Trevor and Sheriff Jacobsen have brought him back yet."

As the two of them talked, Abby became increasingly aware of activity in the hallway and adjoining offices. Though she couldn't make out any words, she heard raised voices, and several people hurried past with intent expressions on their faces. Finally Tracie stood.

"I'm going to see what all the commotion is about."

Abby hovered in the doorway as the other woman approached a nearby Coast Guardsman.

"What's going on?" Tracie's question carried down the hall.

"They're sending another team out to the scene," the Coastie explained briefly.

"To the scene of the accident?" Tracie clarified.

"To the scene of the shooting."

"Shooting?"

"Yes. Didn't you hear? Trevor was bringing in a suspect. When he tried to escape, Trevor shot him. He's dead."

At the Coast Guardsman's explanation, Abby hurried forward. "Shot him? Mitchell Adams is dead?"

"Yes, I believe that was the name of the deceased."

Even as the officer confirmed it, Abby looked down the hall and saw Scott standing in a doorway just beyond her. His expression was hollow. Abby wanted to run to him and throw her arms around him, but he stepped back inside the room and closed the door after him.

Abby looked to Tracie. "Now it's more important than ever that we get that phone. It may be the only link we have to Marilyn and her kidnappers."

Tracie nodded and turned to the Coastie they'd been speaking with. "Gary, have you heard anything about the cell phone Mitchell Adams had been using?"

"Cell phone?" Gary looked thoughtful. "The sheriff was talking about that, too. Seems to me they couldn't find it. Ben and Clint were part of that investigation. I'll give them a call."

"Please do. Let me know right away what you find out." Tracie led Abby back to the office where she'd taken her statement. "That phone *can't* be lost," she muttered.

Abby felt a horrid sense of desperation. "He was on the phone at Greunke's. At least, he was talking to somebody. Maybe I only assumed he was on the phone." She looked up at Tracie. "We need to get back to Greunke's and talk to the waitress. I never actually saw Mitch while I was there, but she did. Maybe he wasn't on the phone. It could have been a radio, or someone could have been there in person, even though I only heard Mitch's voice."

"Sounds like this waitress is the best lead we've got right now," Tracie agreed and looked at her watch. "We've got five minutes before they close at midnight. We'd better hurry."

As the women stepped into the hallway, the door down the hall opened and Scott stepped out. "What are you up to?"

"Tracie and I are going to go talk to the waitress at Greunke's," Abby explained quickly, taking in the frustrated tension that radiated off her friend. "Why don't you come with us?"

"I'm supposed to stick around to identify Mitch's body when they bring him in."

"That won't be for a while," Tracie spoke up. "They'll

have to do a thorough evaluation of the scene. In the meantime, we have to hurry before this waitress leaves work. It won't take long. Why don't you come with us?"

"You know, maybe I should," Scott agreed.

Once Tracie had notified the others that Scott would be leaving with them, Abby and Scott piled into the Coast Guard truck and Tracie drove them the few blocks to Greunke's. Abby extended a tentative hand toward Scott.

He took her hand and squeezed it, though his eyes continued to stare out the window at the spitting sleet.

A moment later, they arrived at Greunke's. Tracie pulled into the graveled parking lot, and they hopped out and hurried toward the front door, where the neon Open sign flickered and died.

Tracie reached the door first, and pulled it open to reveal a startled Deb, keys in hand.

"Sorry, folks, I was just locking up," the waitress apologized.

"Actually, Deb, we'd like to ask you a few questions about a man who was in here earlier," Tracie explained.

Abby stepped forward. "The man with the red Escalade, the one I asked you about when I was in here," she clarified.

"Oh, you mean the guy who ran out without paying?" Deb opened the door a little wider and stood back for them to come inside. "What do you want to know?"

"First of all, can you show us where he was sitting?" Tracie asked.

Deb led them through the restaurant to the farthest dining room. "Right here in this booth, facing this way," Deb explained, showing them a neatly tidied booth. "He ordered the steak and eggs. Barney had to heat up the grill just for him, and then the guy didn't eat half of it before he ran off without paying."

"I'm sorry. How much did he owe you?" Scott asked, pulling out his wallet. "I'll take care of it."

Deb pulled a slip of paper from her apron and passed it to Scott.

"Was anyone else with him?" Tracie pressed.

With a pop of her bubble gum, Deb answered. "He came in with Tim Price, but Tim left before he ordered."

Fear jolted through Abby at Deb's words. Tim Price was Trevor's younger brother. How odd that Tim was the last person Mitch had talked to before his arrest, before Trevor killed him.

"Did you overhear any of their conversation?" Tracie pressed.

The waitress shook her head. "No. They were real quick about it."

"No one else talked to him?" Tracie clarified.

"Not unless you count him talking on his cell phone. He got it out right after I gave him his menu. It looked to me like he tried to call somebody, but he must not have got hold of them, 'cause I no more than got back to rolling silverware than he bellered for me to come take his order. The phone sat right there." Deb touched a spot on the tablecloth. "One of those real tiny new ones that cost so much. You'd think a guy who could afford a phone like that could afford to pay for his steak and eggs."

At the mention of the tab, Scott passed the woman a couple of larger bills. "Keep the change," he murmured.

Abby met his eyes. "He took out his phone when we were on the island, remember? Doesn't that sound like the same phone?"

"Sounds like it," Scott agreed. "And it sounds like something Mitch would carry. He always overspent on the latest technology."

"Was that the only time you saw him use the phone?" Tracie asked.

"Nah. A little later, after she came in—" Deb pointed to Abby "—I went into the kitchen to run a load of dishes." Deb gestured to the kitchen door in plain sight just beyond the lunch counter. Through the window in the door, they had a clear view of the dishwashing equipment. "I saw him pick up his phone again. This time he musta got somebody, but it sure didn't make him any happier. I watched him pretty careful on account of he looked like he might want to hurt somebody, you know? And anybody who hangs out with Tim Price…" She let the words hang in the air, full of suggestion, before she popped another bubble and continued. "And it was a good thing I watched him, 'cause the next thing I knew, he up and ran out. I lit out after him, but he tore off before I even got out the door. Didn't figure a guy in his kinda shape could move that fast."

Tracie nodded as Deb gave her animated account. "Did you see what he did with his phone? He didn't leave it here, did he?"

Deb tipped her head back and laughed. "If he'd left me a fancy phone like that, I wouldn't have been worried about the bill."

"Did he leave anything else behind?" Tracie pressed. "Receipts, scraps of paper, anything?"

"Nope, and I clean up pretty carefully."

"Did he and Tim exchange anything?"

"Not that I saw."

Just then, Tracie's radio came to life. "Tracie, you out there?"

Tracie radioed back in the affirmative.

"Have you still got Scott with you?" A man's voice crackled over the radio.

"Yes," Tracie spoke into the device. "Jim, we need to get somebody over to Tim Price's place. Deb saw him with Mitch just before he chased Abby."

"I'll get some guys right on it," Jim agreed, then drew in a breath loud enough to carry over the radio. "I need you to take Scott on over to the mortuary. The coroner has the body ready for him to identify."

EIGHT

Abby tagged along silently as Tracie drove the three of them across the village to the small funeral home that served as the local mortuary and coroner's office. As the Coast Guard truck came to a stop in the front parking space, Abby said a silent prayer that God would help her find a way to support Scott in the midst of all he was experiencing.

They climbed out of the truck and filed in the front door. Abby had been in the building once before for a neighbor's funeral, but she'd never been past the front parlor and chapel area. Now Earl, the mortician and Bayfield County Coroner, led them down a brightly lit corridor whose unnatural florescent light added a surreal glow to their journey to the exam room. Abby felt a distinct chill as they headed toward the cold room where the body was being held.

Scott didn't like the smell of the mortuary. Too many bad memories—first his grandfather's funeral, then his father's and his grandmother's. The same desperate, hopeless feelings rose up inside him that he'd felt when he'd endured those losses. And now Mitch. He'd never liked the man, but his stepfather's death loomed like a specter over his mother's disappearance. Would she be the next one he came here to identify? Scott couldn't shake the thought from his mind.

The outline under the sheet looked like Mitch. The face, when they peeled back the sheet, was starkly unapologetic, and somehow more real in its expression than the façade Scott had always seen Mitch wear before. He looked away, up to the mortician's somber face, and nodded. "That's him," he said, ready to step back.

As Earl silently pulled the sheet forward again, his slight movement caused Mitch's hand to fall, swinging uselessly back and forth before settling with the fingers pointing downward, as though straining for the floor.

Scott cocked his head to the side. Something didn't look right.

"Where's his ring?" Abby's voice echoed against the stainless steel of the cold exam room. Scott hadn't forgotten she was back there. Though he refused to allow himself to look to her for support, especially knowing she'd endured so much already, he'd taken some comfort in knowing she was with him.

At her comment, Scott realized what wasn't right. A faded white line wrapped around the relative tan of Mitch's left ring finger, stark and indecent in its nakedness. Scott looked to the mortician, half expecting him to explain that he'd already locked away Mitch's valuables.

Instead, Earl answered, "He wasn't wearing any jewelry when I arrived at the scene."

Scott turned to look at Abby, whose expression was one of alarm.

"He was wearing a ring this morning," Abby insisted. "I remember looking at it when we were on the boat, because I wondered if Mitch and your mother were married to each other, and then I noticed how much his ring looked like hers with all the diamonds embedded in it, so I figured they must be."

Scott scowled, trying to remember. He hadn't paid any attention to Mitch's hands all day. He never paid him any more attention than was necessary, preferring to ignore the man when he possibly could. But now it was important. "Did Mitch leave his ring on the boat with the rest of my mother's jewelry?"

At his question, Abby looked at Mitch as though expecting him to sit up and answer. But death had stolen his voice.

"I don't know," Abby admitted. "I wish I had paid more attention."

"I can ask the other Coasties if they noticed Mitch wearing a ring, and have the guys ask Tim Price about it," Tracie offered. "And Deb gave me her home number. Since she remembered Mitch's cell phone so accurately, perhaps she has some recollection of whether he was wearing any jewelry."

Scott agreed. "Perhaps someone will have noticed something." Since there wasn't anything more they could accomplish in the exam room, he thanked the mortician for his time and headed out to the parlor to wait for the paperwork to be completed for his signature. Abby followed him in silence, her solemn expression reminding him of his fears, causing him to wonder again if he wouldn't be back soon to identify his mother. Tracie lingered behind, reviewing the paperwork for the investigation.

The helpless feeling that clutched at him made Scott want to throw his head back and rage at the ceiling in the elaborately appointed front parlor of the funeral home. His mother was out there somewhere, her life in the hands of unknown kidnappers, and his only link to her whereabouts was now dead. He knew he had to do *something* to save his mother. He just didn't know what.

Abby's fingers brushed his arm, her touch almost imperceptibly light. "Did you want to pray?" she asked, her voice hesitant.

He turned to her, his fear boiling over. Death had been inching closer to them all day, and had now come too close. "Pray? I've been doing that all day and things have only gone from bad to worse." Before she could answer, he continued. "Why don't you get out of here before something happens to you? This isn't about you. It's about me finding my mother. You don't need to get any more caught up in it."

It wasn't until Abby dropped his hand and took a step back, her expression pained, that Scott realized how his words must have sounded. He'd actually been thinking that she needed to get away from him for her own protection, but that certainly wasn't the way his words had come out. "I just don't want—" he started.

But Abby had already moved toward the door.

"Abby, I—" he started again, just as Tracie came in from the back room.

"Well, we're at an impasse." She sighed as she clipped her radio back into its case at her belt. "Tim Price wasn't home." Then she looked from Scott and Abby and blinked. "Am I interrupting something?"

"No, it's okay," Abby reached for the doorknob and opened it. "I was just headed home. I don't think there's anything more I can do for you tonight."

"Oh." Tracie looked mildly concerned, but then shrugged. "Well, I've got your contact information if we need you, so I guess that's okay."

Abby nodded and slipped out the door.

"Abby." Scott started after her. He got as far as the open doorway and then stopped. The sleet had changed to hard, pebblelike snow. Abby hurried up the hill, presumably toward home. Scott didn't know where she lived. He realized there was a lot about her he didn't know. He didn't know why he felt such a strong connection to her after just one day. And he certainly didn't know how he was going to make things right with her after the way he'd just spoken to her.

With a sigh, Scott took one last look at Abby's fading figure as she hurried off into the night. Then he stepped back inside the mortuary and closed the door. He had things to do. He needed to sign the papers identifying his stepfather's body. And then he needed to find his mother, before she ended up in the same place.

"I got in touch with Deb," Tracie continued as though nothing had happened. "She was able to recall that Mitch had been wearing a ring at the restaurant, even after Tim Price left, but she couldn't describe what the ring looked like."

"Does she need to be able to describe it?"

"To prove in court that she saw him wearing it, yes. But for our purposes, it's enough to assume Mitch was wearing the ring at the restaurant, and therefore, presumably, at the time of his death." Tracie explained as Earl entered the room, paperwork in hand.

Scott pressed, "So somebody took it from his body after he died?"

"Presumably."

"Why? And who?" Scott's head was beginning to spin from all the strange details of the case. It had to mean something—but why would someone stoop to petty thievery once Mitch was already dead?

Earl spoke up. "Tracie asked me the same question moments ago. There were four investigators at the scene. We both know all four of them."

As the quiet man's voice drifted to silence, Tracie added, "They're solid guys, but right now, they're also our only suspects as far as the ring goes."

"Four guys," Scott repeated.

"Yes. And of course, Trevor," Earl pointed out.

"Of course." Scott nearly choked. "The guy who killed Mitch in the first place." His eyes narrowed. "And he was alone with the body before any of the investigators arrived, whereas they would have all had each other as witnesses the entire time they were at the scene, am I right?"

Earl was completely silent, his expression somber. Tracie made some notes on her paperwork, but didn't answer immediately. When she looked up, her words sounded slightly out of place. "Trevor is my Coast Guard partner. I trust him every day with my life."

"So you're saying he's trustworthy?" Scott pressed.

"I need to get back to headquarters," Tracie responded flatly.

Earl presented them both with the documents he held. "Please sign these papers before you go."

Abby felt completely rotten when she arrived at home, and vowed never to drink coffee on an empty stomach again. The whole day had been far too overwhelming. She hadn't even known Mitch twenty-four hours before. Now he was dead.

Two messages blinked on her machine. One from her sister, one from her mom, something about Thanksgiving plans, and did she still have her recipe for apple-raspberry pie? Abby listened to their mechanically captured voices in the emptiness of her kitchen and she hugged herself, glad her family was safe and accounted for. Then she choked back a sob for Scott and his mother and all the uncertainties that surrounded them.

She wished there was something she could do to help. She'd always adored Scott back in college, and would have jumped at the chance to spend time with him back then. But now as then, he evaded her, his world bigger and busier and somehow more important than the mundane simplicities that occupied her. He had to rescue his mother from heartless killers. She had to find her recipe for apple-raspberry pie. They lived in two completely different worlds. She would do well to remember that.

By rights, she knew she ought to leave Scott alone. She had no claim on his life, on the search for his mother, on any of it. If he'd have asked her to help him search, she'd have gone to the ends of the earth and back again if she'd have thought it would help bring his mother back, or even simply bring him some measure of comfort in Marilyn's absence. But he hadn't asked for her help. He'd asked her to stay away.

She fixed herself a bowl of cereal to settle her stomach. So much had gone wrong, and it churned inside her as she struggled to sort it all out. Trevor wanted his ring back. Trevor shot Mitch. Trevor's brother went to Greunke's with Mitch. Tim. Tim Price.

Abby's spoon settled in the empty bowl in front of her as her mind drifted back in time. Trevor's little brother Tim had been a close pal of hers once, the little brother she'd never had. Though the Price family had never been churchgoing folks, Abby had dragged Trevor with her when she'd gone to services while they were dating. And Tim had tagged along of his own volition. Abby had even convinced him to spend a week at the Christian camp she'd grown up attending.

It was her understanding that Tim had become a Christian at camp. He'd certainly come away a changed person. For a few years, she'd looked back and figured Tim's salvation was the one redemptive thing she'd gotten out of her whole rotten relationship with Trevor.

But lately it seemed Tim had fallen in with the wrong crowd. She'd heard rumors about him drinking and even using drugs. Though a part of her had wanted to talk to him and try to help him out, she'd been too scared of getting back in touch with the Trevor era of her life to ever follow through with him.

What had Tim gotten himself into now? Was he beyond reaching?

Abby blinked and sat up with a start. She'd almost dozed off for a moment, exhausted and lost in thought. But now she knew exactly what she needed to do. She needed to talk to Tim. Now. And though the Coast Guard guys had been unable to find him, she suddenly realized where he was most likely to be.

The Brick wasn't like any of the downtown pubs, which were brightly lit and eccentrically decorated to lure in the tourist crowd. The shady bar was a magnet for illegal activity, half-hidden at the end of an alley on a bluff near the edge of town, and could have easily been mistaken for someone's crumbling old garage if not for the neon signs advertising cheap beer. Like a cinderblock plunked down by a giant, The Brick nestled in next to the hillside, reminding Abby of Mrs. Frisby's home in Nimh.

Abby had never been inside The Brick, but now was not

a time for cowardice. She was long overdue for a talk with Tim. Besides that, it was the only way she knew to help Scott find his mother, the only lead she had in her hands to pursue. So she really had no choice.

The rusting metal door opened on well-greased hinges, and Abby blinked at the smoky fog of the dim interior. A couple of grizzled fishermen sat at the bar, but otherwise, the place appeared to be empty. Then Abby heard the clink of balls near the back and saw Tim bent over the lone pool table, playing a game all by himself.

Reminding herself that the younger man had once looked up to her, even held her in awe as a beloved older sister, Abby drummed up the courage to proceed. "Tim?" She blinked at him and smiled her friendliest smile, as though running into him was a happy coincidence. "Tim Price?"

When Tim looked up and met her eyes, Abby realized how very overdue their conversation was. Though he stood nearly as tall as his brother, his skin clung to his skeletal frame, and his eyes bulged out from sunken hollows, gaunt and haunted. Where once there had been light and life and promise, now there were only shadows, as though his soul had been stolen by the powder and drink.

"Abby?" A faraway smile stole across his features, and for an instant, she recognized the young man she'd once known. "What are you doing here?"

She shrugged. "Thought I might play some pool."

"Well, have at it." Discordant laughter bubbled from his mouth. Though she had no personal experience with alcohol, she could tell he was wasted.

Abby nodded and took hold of a pool cue. She'd get through this, somehow. And when Marilyn was finally rescued, she'd see that Tim got some help.

* * *

Scott stepped into the seedy joint he'd seen Abby enter, and looked around, aghast that she'd venture inside such a place. He'd looked her up in the phone book and had Tracie give him a lift to her place so he could try to apologize. They'd pulled up just in time to see her disappear around the corner on foot. Scott had followed at a distance, wondering what she was up to.

He wondered even more now. But when he heard the name Tim Price floating through the smoke as she approached the man in back, Scott decided he could hold back his fears for her safety for a little while longer. He ducked into a booth close enough to the pool table that he could overhear Abby's conversation with Tim. When Abby glanced up and saw him, Scott lifted a finger to his lips, motioning for her to keep quiet about his presence.

An understanding smile flickered across her face, but she didn't pause in her conversation. Fortunately it seemed Tim was one of those guys who liked to talk when he was drunk.

"The Coast Guard job is chicken feed." Tim's voice warbled. "It keeps him in the know, is all. He's got clout, that's why they let him in on the big deals."

"Like this one?" Abby prompted. Scott watched her try to shoot pool with Tim, but from what he could see, it didn't appear as though she'd ever held a pool cue before. Tim, however, appeared to be wasted enough not to notice her obvious lack of skill.

"Yeah, some land development deal. Big chunk of property. They just have to take care of the owners, you know, 'cause they didn't want to sell."

"Take care of them?" Abby prompted.

"Yeah, you know, get 'em out of the picture so they can

take possession. They've got this guy Mitch. *Idiot.* He was supposed to help them, but he's getting in the way. What he doesn't know is, they don't even need him anymore."

"They don't?"

"Nope. Got it all taken care of." Tim chuckled, sounding pleased with himself.

Scott felt his heart sink. What had been taken care of? Was his mother already dead?

"So what about the jewelry?" Abby asked. "Was that just a cover?"

Scott stiffened. Abby's question had come out of nowhere. He hadn't heard Tim say anything about jewelry yet. But maybe Abby figured Tim was so out of it he wouldn't notice.

Her guess seemed to be a good one. Tim just kept right on chuckling.

"The jewelry!" He slapped his knee and gripped his pool stick for support as his laughter bent him double. "That was just too easy. Too easy!" he repeated.

His loud antics drew a glare from the fishermen at the bar. Tim looked up, saw their expressions and sidled closer to Abby. Scott had to strain to hear.

"They've been running diamonds through those islands for years. That's how Trevor got in with them, see. He keeps the Coast Guard out of their way, makes it nice and smooth for them, gets his cut, no questions, right? That's how they paid this Mitch guy. Diamonds. He uses them to lure this woman, then has her leave the diamonds on the boat. Bingo! They get their diamonds back, got the woman *and* the land *and* the evidence, and nobody's none the wiser."

"Wow." Abby nodded, playing right along. "That's brilliant."

"You betcha. And the best part? They ain't even diamonds."

"They're not?"

"Nope. They're all the same. Syn-thet-ics." He sounded the word out slowly, as though he might not have been able to spit it out any other way. "Only problem is, now the feds are trying to trace them back here. Trevor's got to tie up his loose ends. Getting into real estate now, 'cause the gig is up on the diamonds."

"They need them back?" Abby repeated. "Is that why Trevor wants his ring back?"

"Yup." Tim nodded. "Yup, yup, yup." His voice faded. Then his eyes seemed to focus and he looked at Abby as though for the first time. "Oh, Abby." He shook his head. "Abby, you shouldn't ought to be here."

Cold dread slid down Scott's spine. He needed to get Abby out of there, and fast.

The fisherman at the bar looked antsy, their attention obviously focused on Tim and Abby's conversation.

"You know, I probably should go. Thanks for the game, Tim," Abby called. She swept over and grabbed Scott's hand, whisking him off to the door.

The last thing he heard before the door slammed behind them was Tim's warbling voice, now frantic, as he shouted, "We can't let them get away!"

NINE

"Run!" Abby screamed to Scott as she pulled him by the hand through the mud-and-gravel parking lot. She'd seen coherence hit Tim's eyes the second he'd realized what he'd told her. Tim had always cared too deeply about what Trevor thought of him. If he thought he'd betrayed his brother's confidence, who knew what he might do?

Though Abby had been the first one out the door, Scott's long legs quickly carried him past her. He held tight to her hand, and by the time they reached the edge of the parking lot, he was pulling her.

"Hurry," he encouraged her in a low voice as the door to The Brick opened behind them.

A quick glance back told Abby that all three men had come out after them. She choked back a scream and scrambled forward over the uneven ground, hardly noticing the thick layer of ice that coated the ground after a night of freezing rain. She feared the men behind her far more than she feared falling down.

The side of the bluff fell away in front of them in a steep track of overgrown sidewalk. Scott paused for a second in front of her, but before she could stop herself, her forward momentum carried her sliding into his back.

He tipped forward unsteadily, threw his weight backward, and their feet shot out from under them on the slick ice. They skidded down the bluff in a tangle of legs and flailing arms.

Abby tried to grab hold of something, to gain some measure of control over her path, but the slick ice coated everything. She wanted to scream, but didn't dare give away their position to the men who followed them.

The men's voices carried through the night.

"Where'd they go?"

"Down the hill!"

"I don't see them."

"There! On the sidewalk!"

"Not on foot, you idiot. We'll take the truck. They won't get far."

An engine roared to life above them as Abby and Scott continued their out-of-control slide down the steep incline. With an angry bump, Abby's hip rammed into the side of the curb where a street bisected the slope.

Scott gained his feet and tried to pull her up. "Come on, hurry. They're right behind us."

Abby managed to get one knee hooked over the curb before her leg slid sideways and knocked Scott's feet out from under him. He landed half on top of her, sending them both skidding downward again. She flung her arms out, grasping for a hold as the incline steepened further and they hurtled downward with increasing speed.

"Hold on!" Scott fingers wrapped around hers, and though they continued to shoot down the hillside, he somehow got her tucked between his knees, with his arms wrapped safely around her shoulders, positioned as though they were riding a toboggan. But instead of a solid sled beneath them, the seats of their jeans shot across the ice, every bump and rut jarring their legs, bruising them as they went.

The sound of an accelerating engine echoed across the bluff above them, and Abby realized just how close their pursuers were. With a jolt, they skidded to a stop at the next curb, and Abby looked up to see the church.

"Hurry." Scott pitched them forward again, but the ground leveled on the church's lot, and though they skidded crazily on their hands and knees, they no longer moved forward with any speed. "We're sitting ducks. We've got to get out of here," Scott hissed at her as he lunged himself off the sidewalk and onto the church lawn.

Abby rolled forward until she reached the grass. Though every blade bore a thick coating of ice, the uneven surface gave her some measure of traction after the smooth slickness of the sidewalk and street. "This way," she shouted, scrambling sideways across the churchyard.

With a minimum of slipping and sliding, they scuttled past the church to the edge of the steep ravine that cut through the west side of the lot. Abby paused for a second and looked down at the jagged ice-covered rocks. Her tender legs cried out in protest after all the bruises she'd bought with her trip down the bluff. But then headlights flashed in front of them as the truck made the corner at the top of the street.

"Down!" Abby cried, stepping off into the darkness and landing with a skidding thump on her rear. Beside her, Scott descended more or less on his feet. He reached the bottom of the forty-foot ravine and pulled her after him toward the storm drain that ran beneath the street.

"Duck," he urged as he leaned toward the dark opening. Abby balked. "No," she whimpered, blinking at the blackness. "Anything could be in there. Do you want to wake a hibernating bear?"

"We don't have a choice," Scott whispered intently at her ear. He tugged on her arm.

Above them, the truck screeched to a halt and the men's voices rang through the night.

"Where'd they go?"

"I saw them by the church."

"Check the ravine!"

Abby realized she had no other choice. She pressed her cheek to Scott's warm flannel shirt and ducked with him into the darkness.

The space was tight, the metal freezing cold against their backs, the voices above them much too close. At any moment, Abby fully expected a badger to attack them from the darkness, or Tim's crazed face to appear in the opening before them. She pinched her eyes shut and waited.

Scott's chest rose and fell beneath her cheek as he sucked in huge silent breaths. She clung to him as though somehow, by just holding him tightly enough, she could ward off everyone who hunted them. Her mind swarmed with fear and prayers as she asked God to make them invisible, to blind the eyes of their pursuers, and shield them from danger.

"I'm not going down there. I'll break my neck." A thick Wisconsin brogue echoed off the rocks as the beam of a flashlight bounced through the ravine.

"I don't see them anyway."

"So what did they do? I didn't see what happened."

"They know things." Tim's voice stuttered uncertainly. "They know things they shouldn't know."

"You and your conspiracy theories," the other voice followed. "Here I thought they were some of Sal's guys."

"Sal's guys?" the brogue chided. "Nah. Sal don't work with girls or pretty boys."

The voices faded and a moment later, Abby heard truck doors slamming.

Though her breathing slowed, she still clutched tightly at Scott's quilted flannel shirt. A shudder chased up and down her spine as she considered how close they'd come to capture. She sucked in a trembling breath.

"What was that, Abby?" Scott's lips skirted her hairline as he whispered close to her ear. "What were you doing up there?"

She twitched a tiny shrug. "I could see the wheels turning in Tim's mind. I knew at any moment he'd realize he shouldn't be talking to me. I had to ask him. I couldn't beat around the bush any longer. I had to know."

Scott's hands made their way up her back and pressed her tighter against him as he spoke. "But why did you even go into that place? What were you thinking?"

She pulled away from him slightly and tried to look at him, but the darkness inside the drain was too deep for her to see anything but the tiniest glint off his eyes. "I thought we needed answers. And we got some."

"But at what cost?" Scott pressed.

"We know what they're after now, don't we?"

"They're after *us*."

"They want the rings. And the land." Abby closed her eyes and rested her head against Scott's strong shoulder. She felt so tired and sore. "Did you hear what Tim said? They've been smuggling in fake diamonds and passing them off as the real thing for years. Only now someone's figured out what they've got, and they have to cover their tracks. That's why Trevor wants his ring back—because if the authorities knew where it came from, it would lead them straight to him."

"And you could do the same thing, Abby."

"Do what?"

"Lead the authorities to Trevor."

Abby swallowed. "I will. I don't owe him anything. I'll tell Tracie everything I know. I've got the ring in my pocket right now. She can have it. It's evidence."

Scott shook his head slowly behind her. "If Trevor finds out you know what you have, he'll come after you. He killed Mitch, he'll kill you."

"He doesn't know I know."

"Tim may have been drunk, but he could still remember what he told you."

"Yeah, but he won't tell his brother that he ratted him out. Tim *adores* Trevor. He'd never expose his own failure to him."

"He adored his brother five years ago, you mean. You don't know that's still the case."

Abby sucked in her breath through her teeth. Scott had a good point. "It doesn't matter," she protested. "Tim won't tell Trevor. He's not that stupid."

"Isn't he?" Scott's arms tightened around her. "Abby, you can't go home. It's not safe. We've got to get you out of here."

Abby pulled back and looked him full in the face in spite of the darkness that cloaked his features in blackness. "We've got to find your mother, you mean."

"Not *we*," Scott corrected. "*I* have to find my mother. You need to get out of here. It's too dangerous."

"It's too dangerous for me, but not for you?"

"Yes!"

"Why?"

Scott didn't answer.

Abby pushed herself out of the storm drain and stood. "This is ridiculous. Fine. You want me out of here? I'm out of here."

"Wait." Scott crawled out after her. "Abby, be sensible."

She turned to face him and hissed in a half-shouting whisper, "I *am* being sensible. It's the middle of the night. Tim's too drunk to make it back to the bar by himself, let alone find his brother and rat me out. If Trevor wanted to come after me he's had plenty of time to do it, but I still have his ring and until he gets it back, I don't think he dares do anything to hurt me. So I'm going home and going to bed, since obviously you don't want or need my help." She tried to stalk off, but between the rough-cut rocks and the ice, she didn't make it very far.

"At least let me walk you home," Scott insisted, placing a steadying hand at her back.

"Fine." She wiped a tear away quickly before he could see. And then she let him walk her home in silence. She didn't trust her voice to speak, though she wanted terribly to ask him why he could offer help to her but wouldn't allow her to help him.

Scott felt strange sleeping in the room his mother and stepfather had reserved at the Seagull Bay Motel, but since it was the only room he could get in the wee hours of the morning, he lay down on the bed that smelled of his mother and begged God to let him see her again. After the rough way he'd left Abby, his mother was the only person he had left in the world. He couldn't allow himself to lose her, though at the same time, he knew he had to prepare his heart for that very real possibility.

Mitch was dead. The very thought sickened him, especially when he considered the possibility that Mitch may have been the last link he had to his mother's whereabouts. For having never liked the man, Scott still felt remorseful that he'd died, and betrayed that the man had been in cahoots with the diamond smugglers all along. He couldn't imagine how his mother would respond. He prayed he'd have the opportunity to tell her.

His body ached. Several bruises were rising up from his trip down the bluff and the tumble over the brownstone ledge, and his arms and shoulders cried out in pain from the exertion of rowing the canoe. The day had been long, and morning was only a few hours away.

But he couldn't sleep. His mind continued to turn over scenes—seeing Mitch through the cold tinted windows of the sheriff's patrol car, seeing his mother for the last time as she'd stood on the pier waving goodbye to him as he set off for Rocky Island. And Abby.

The problem was, Abby was right. The only reason he didn't want her helping was because he was afraid she'd get hurt. But he was just as likely to get hurt without her help, quite possibly more so. He already owed her his life at least twice over. She'd rescued him from Devil's Island, and alerted him to the problem with his brakes before it had caused an accident.

Through it all she'd been sweet, even funny at times, courageous, creative, strong. All qualities he looked for in a woman. And she worked for the Eagle Foundation so he knew that, unlike Mitch, she'd share his vision for conserving the land he'd inherited. Once again, he felt guilty when he recalled how little he'd told her about the land. After all she'd done, Abby had a right to know the rest of the story.

He'd shortchanged her. He'd done what he'd always done, fallen into the same pattern his fellow Christian counselors at the office always pointed out when he broke up with a girlfriend. He'd refused to allow himself to be vulnerable. He'd refused to let her help him. When he'd felt himself drawing close to her, he'd held back. Worst of all, when he'd felt himself falling for her, he'd pushed her away.

Though he loved his job as a counselor and lived for helping others, Scott resented the way his knowledge of human nature gave him insights into his own behavior. Because he knew what he was doing was wrong. He could have been happily married years ago if he hadn't worked so hard to chase caring women like Abby out of his life. But this time the stakes were much higher. Abby wasn't just a sweet girl like the other women he'd dated.

Abby was someone very special. He'd been attracted to her back in college, and he'd never quite forgotten her. She'd openly expressed her feelings, opinions and faith through the poems she'd written for the class they shared, and Scott had always respected and admired her convictions. Through God's grace, she was back in his life again. Miracles like that didn't happen every day.

But instead of thanking God for bringing her back into his life, he was pushing Abby away. Though he'd told himself he was only concerned for her safety, deep down, he knew there was more to it. He didn't want to see her get hurt, but he didn't want to be hurt by her, either. Losing his grandparents and his father had hurt him. Losing Abby just when he'd found her again was a blow he didn't know if he'd be strong enough to take.

He was left with a choice he didn't want to have to make. He could move back into his comfort zone and push her away. It was what he'd always done, retreating to the comfort of God, who he knew would never forsake him, whenever a friend moved away or a loved one died—especially when his grandparents and his father had passed away. Or he could take the greater risk and allow Abby into his heart.

At the very thought, he felt the blood pumping fiercely through his veins and he gripped the tangled bedsheets. How could he let Abby get close to him—assuming she'd even condescend to speak to him again after the cold way he'd treated her earlier? What if she rejected him? What if she was killed? Then he'd be more alone than ever before, and with only a broken heart to show for it.

Shaking off those fears, he snapped on the bedside lamp and fumbled about in the nightstand drawer until his fingers found what he wanted. A Bible.

Flipping it open, he quickly found the verses from Ecclesiastes that he'd used so many times in counseling sessions with engaged and married couples.

Two are better than one, because they have a good return for their work:

If one falls down, his friend can help him up.

But pity the man who falls and has no one to help him up!

Also, if two lie down together, they will keep warm.

But how can one keep warm alone?

Though one may be overpowered, two can defend themselves.

The ancient words burned into his mind as he stared at them, speaking to him with the authority of God's own voice. He was alone, with no one to help him up, no one to warm him, no one at his back to defend him.

The words spoke to him like a promise. *Though one may be overpowered, two can defend themselves.*

The longer he stared at the text, the more certain Scott became that he wouldn't be able to rescue his mother by himself. But with Abby on his side, they could at least hope to keep each other safe. Though the emotional risks involved still intimidated him, he knew his only hope was to be reconciled with Abby, and to ask her—to beg her, if necessary—to help him continue the search.

He rolled over onto his side and clutched the extra bed pillow. "Dear God," he whispered into the darkness, "I know what I need to do, but I don't know if I can do it. I need Your help."

TEN

Abby filed into her usual pew and flipped absently through the Sunday worship bulletin, her eyes blurring over song titles and announcements, unseeing. Prayer concerns and upcoming events jumbled together, but all she could think about was Scott and his mother.

Poor Marilyn. She was out there somewhere, almost certainly hungry, cold and afraid. Probably hurting. Possibly even dead. Abby wanted more than anything to be out there searching for her, but she knew Scott didn't want her help. His rejection stung, not only because of her feelings for him, but because she'd believed she could contribute to Marilyn's rescue. But Scott must not have thought so, or else he would have let her help.

As she'd mulled over Mitch's words the night before, Abby had concluded that Marilyn's captors most likely had taken her out to Devil's Island again, awaiting Mitch's signal, waiting to kill her. Unless, as they'd clearly threatened Mitch, they'd jumped the gun and disposed of her already. Abby shifted uncomfortably in her seat at the thought.

The people around her stood. It took Abby a moment to realize the worship service had started. Everyone else was singing. She found the words and lent her voice halfheartedly, praying the whole time that God would be with Marilyn, and that God would be with Scott.

Scott. At the thought of him, her eyes blurred over. No, she wouldn't cry during worship. She sniffed and returned her attention to the music, refusing to glance to the right or the left.

So it wasn't until she sat down after the song that she noticed the figure who'd joined her at the end of her pew.

Scott.

The minister was praying, so Abby quickly closed her eyes and focused her heart. She didn't hear the words that were spoken as much as the cry of her heart. Scott had come to worship? He was sitting by her? Did it mean anything, or was it just a lucky coincidence?

The minister concluded the prayer, then spoke the same words he said every Sunday morning. "Just as through Christ we have been reconciled to God, so let us also be reconciled to one another, and share the peace of Christ."

Abby stood. This was the part of the service when everyone shook hands with one another as a gesture of reconciliation. They were supposed to say something formal like "peace be with you," while looking solemn, but more often, the good friends of the church hugged each other and used the time to chat and greet their neighbors.

By the time Abby dared to look his way, Scott had stepped toward her, one hand outstretched. "Peace," he said softly, his eyes riveted on hers and brimming with meaning.

Though she nearly choked on the word, Abby managed to utter a soft "peace," as she took his hand. It wasn't until he pulled her into his embrace that she let a tear escape.

They sat through the service side by side, and Scott kept his hand on hers during the sermon. Abby wanted to ask why he wasn't out looking for his mother, but there was no time to talk, and she realized that, pressing as the search might be, they wouldn't get anywhere without God on their side. Worshipping Him was the most important thing they could do.

After the service, she and Scott ducked out the side door before any of her church friends had a chance to catch up to her. She didn't know what Scott's plan was, but she knew if she got to talking with her friends they'd waste valuable time.

When they reached the sidewalk, Scott turned to face her and spoke openly for the first time. "I'm sorry I pushed you away last night."

The words soothed her like salve on a wound. "It's okay, Scott. You've been under enormous stress. I understand."

"Still, it was no excuse for me to speak to you the way I did." Scott took her gloved hands in his. "I appreciate all the help you've been. If it weren't for you, I'd still be stuck on that island, maybe even dead right now."

Warmth crept up Abby's cheeks. "I just did what anyone else would do."

"No." Scott shook his head. "No one else could have done what you did. God put you on that boat with me for a reason. Abby, you know that island as well as anyone. You're my best hope for finding my mother alive. I know I have no right to ask this of you, but will you help me continue the search?"

"Of course." She beamed at him, so grateful that he wanted her help.

The words were no sooner out of her mouth than Scott leaned forward and planted a gentle kiss on her cheek. "Thank you." He met her eyes, his expression infinitely tender. "Thank you so much, Abby. You've given me hope."

Touched by his gesture, it took Abby a moment to find words. "We should probably get moving, then. Do you have a plan for this morning?"

Scott cleared his throat. "I called over to the Coast Guard Station after I left you at your place last night, and told them what we'd learned from Tim. They're going to call Trevor and hold him until they can look into Tim's story about the diamond smugglers."

"Did you tell them about my ring?" She suddenly felt self-conscious about her connection to the smugglers, however innocent her involvement had been.

"There were so many details to discuss, and I didn't want to get part of your story wrong and send them off in the wrong direction. The ring is yours. It's up to you to decide when and how you want to tell them about it."

Though Abby had intended to hand over the ring from the moment she'd discovered its connection to the case, she felt touched by Scott's thoughtfulness. "Thank you."

Scott continued. "They also filled me in on what else they've learned. Kermit Hendrickson, Mom's accountant, was able to reach most of my mother's credit card companies, but none of them have had any activity in the past twenty-four hours. Also, one of the guys who accompanied Mitch back to the mainland remembered him wearing a ring and described it accurately, so we know he didn't leave his wedding band aboard the *Helene*. Of course, from what you learned from Tim last night, my guess is Trevor took the ring after he shot Mitch, because it was made with the diamonds they've been smuggling. And there's still no sign of his cell phone—no doubt Trevor took that, too—so we have no leads on who he was talking to or where they might be."

"So where does that leave us?" Abby asked, quickly absorbing all the information Scott had dumped on her.

"I believe our biggest clue to my mom's whereabouts right now was the conversation you overheard at Greunke's last night. What's your impression? Do you think my mom is on the mainland, or back out at Devil's Island?"

"Devil's Island," Abby answered without hesitation. "I don't know exactly what Mitch intended, but he sounded like he was trying to press them to wait for his signal and they didn't want to wait. No matter what that signal was supposed to be for, if they haven't heard from him they almost assuredly would move ahead with their plans by now." Abby intentionally avoided any mention of what those plans were. She didn't want to consider the possibility that Marilyn might already be dead.

"Then that's where we're going."

His sure tone surprised her. "So you trust me?"

As Scott looked down at her, his determined expression softened. "You're all I have left right now. I can't afford to *not* trust you." He slung one strong arm around her shoulders and pulled her into a hug.

Abby smiled as, in spite of the brisk October wind, Scott's words warmed her. It wasn't exactly a profession of love, but it was more than she'd dared to hope for. "Let's stop by the Coast Guard Station and see if we can catch a boat out."

They drove the eight blocks to the Coast Guard Station and arrived as Tracie Crandall was carrying a mesh bag of cold-weather kayaking gear to a utility boat.

"I thought your shift was over," Scott accused.

Letting the bag she carried drop to the ground, Tracie put her hands on her hips. "My partner shot your stepdad last night, and your mother is still missing. You think I could sleep? Besides, this is shaping up to be a pretty big deal. They've called in more help, and they're asking people to work double shifts."

"Have you heard anything new since last night?"

Tracie sighed. "Trevor's missing."

"Missing?" Abby and Scott repeated simultaneously.

"He's not at home, he's not answering any calls. We've been completely unable to find him," Tracie explained.

"So you have no way of corroborating Tim's story?" Abby asked.

"We know a few things," Tracie said. "When Trevor brought Mitch in last night, he came alone. Sheriff Jacobsen stayed at the crash site. The sheriff was the initial responding officer, so it was his job to brief the investigation team on what had happened. But what that means is, Trevor was alone with Mitch long enough to take the ring. He also doesn't have a witness to confirm that Mitch was really attempting to escape when he shot him."

Though she'd already concluded that Trevor had murdered Mitch, hearing Tracie speak the words out loud made the crime seem even more real. "We've got to hurry up and find Marilyn," Abby breathed.

Scott asked Tracie, "How soon are you headed out to the island?"

"As soon as I can get this equipment loaded."

"Mind if we head out with you?"

Tracie picked up the mesh bag again and tossed it to him. "Help me load the boat. I'll make sure we have enough kayaks for the two of you." Then she looked at the long wool skirt Abby wore. "You might want to change first."

"We need to pick up a quick lunch, too," Scott added.

Abby agreed. She still felt hungry from the missed

meals the day before. "How about if I run home, change clothes, grab us some sandwiches and then meet you guys back here?"

"Perfect."

Scott helped Tracie load the rest of the equipment they might need, including extra radios so he and Abby could communicate with the others. Extra Coast Guardsmen had arrived and joined them on the boat. Now, Scott hunkered down next to Abby as they headed out into the cold open sea.

Though the wind had stopped blowing and the sun occasionally peeked through the clouds, the temperature had turned decidedly bitter. Scott was glad for the excuse to sit close to Abby. He had a lot he wanted to tell her, and he was able to keep the conversation that much more private by making it appear as though they were merely cuddling and sharing the sandwiches and trail mix she'd brought.

"I'm sorry I took your mom's spot on the canoe," Abby apologized as soon as he sat down.

"What?" The regret in her tone confused him.

"If I hadn't been on the canoe, your mother would have gone with you to Rocky Island. She'd be safe. I could have stayed on Devil's and kept an eye on Mitch. He didn't have any incentive to harm me. I would have been there when the Coast Guard arrived, and your mother wouldn't be missing. Everything would be fine."

Her apology tore at his heart, especially after the way he'd spoken to her the night before. "No, Abby, it wouldn't. First of all, my mother never would have made it to Rocky Island. She's a pretty hearty gal for her age, but she's not nearly as strong as you are. Besides, even if we had made it across, if the Coast Guard had rescued us, we never would have found out about Mitch and his plans to kill us. He just would have found another way. My mother and I would still be in danger, but we wouldn't even realize it."

"You think so?" Abby mused reflectively.

"Yeah. I do." Scott sighed.

"But last night you said—" Abby began.

Scott took her hand as she reached into the bag of trail mix they shared between them. "I know what I said, and I'm sorry. You've been a tremendous help, and I never should have pushed you away. I just—" he squeezed her hand a little more firmly "—I was scared. So much happened so quickly, and I had to depend on you…it frightened me. In my experience, if I depend too much on someone, they die."

Abby's eyes widened.

"My grandfather was my best friend when I was a teenager. Dad and I didn't see eye-to-eye on a lot of things, but Grandpa was always there for me. He kept me grounded. Then when he died, I realized how fragile life is, and I reconciled with my father." Scott's voice wavered as he stepped back into that guarded past he'd tried so hard to put behind him.

"And then your father died," Abby finished softly.

Scott nodded. He was glad she understood. "I know in my head that caring for a person doesn't make them die. But on a purely instinctual, self-defensive level, I tend to push people away when they get too close. That's what I was doing with you last night, and it wasn't fair to you."

Abby patted the hand that held hers. "It's okay. I was pretty spooked by everything, too. It's a lot to take in all at once."

Her confession made Scott smile. He appreciated that

she was secure enough to comfort him, even after he'd been unfair to her. After dealing with his mother's insecurities, he found Abby's strength reassuring, and very attractive.

"You saved my life."

He felt Abby shudder next to him. "I still can't get over the way Mitch behaved. He was so angry when I overheard him talking on the phone. But I guess more things make sense now—like why he thought you should try swimming to Rocky Island."

"He knew I'd never make it."

"Perhaps he even thought he could convince your mom to jump in and save you."

"He would think that." Scott scowled at his sandwich. "He was always able to manipulate her far too easily. I'm sure he's why she was foolish enough to wear her jewelry on the boat—and then to turn around and leave it all with Captain Sal."

Abby frowned. "It's all so calculated, so cold. And then to turn around and sabotage your car—I can hardly believe he did that."

"As far as that goes, you can believe it. Before he married my mother, Mitch was co-owner of a large used-car dealership. He certainly knew his way around cars. And, though I tried not to listen to any of them, I've heard rumors about some shady practices related to his dealership. For my mom's sake, I had hoped they weren't true. But now that I think about it, I can begin to see the pattern in his personality, some of the things he said over the years…" Scott watched the islands slip by as Tracie steered the boat through their maze toward Devil's.

"Like what?" Abby asked.

"Like his insistence on developing the land my mother

and I had inherited. He thought we were crazy to put the land into a conservation easement—"

"The land's under easement?" Abby broke in, her voice excited.

"Not yet," Scott said with a smile. Somehow he'd known she'd share his opinion on the easement. "We were in the final stages of the process. As I'm sure you know, it can be a lengthy one."

"I *do* know. But once the land goes into easement, it can't be developed—not even by future owners."

"Exactly." Scott gave her hand a squeeze. "That's why it makes sense that Mitch would be in a hurry to get me and Mom out of the picture before the easement goes through."

"In enough of a hurry that he'd resort to desperate behavior." Abby squinted her eyes with comprehension.

"The kind of desperate behavior that got him killed," Scott finished for her.

"I still have trouble accepting the fact that Trevor shot him. I mean, I knew as well as anyone that he wasn't a very nice guy. But to be involved in all this, and then to shoot Mitch."

"I feel the same way about Mitch," Scott agreed. "I never liked him, but even when everything started to point to him, I still had trouble believing he'd stoop so low. I guess familiarity breeds trust, even when it's completely unfounded."

"You're probably right." Abby made a face. "And to be honest, I'm not entirely surprised. Trevor's one of the few people in this world who I can actually imagine killing someone in cold blood. He just has a sinister personality."

As the boat made headway through the maze of islands, Scott considered Abby's words. She sounded as though she'd accepted that Trevor's act hadn't been accidental. But at the same time, her words didn't sound vengeful like those of other scorned lovers he'd counseled. No, she simply sounded as though she knew Trevor well enough to see past his façade. "It always puzzled me that you dated him in college."

Once again, Abby shuddered, and her shiver radiated through their thick coats, causing Scott's own spine to tingle. "I didn't know who he was," Abby mused aloud. "That's part of why I find him so disturbing. When we first met, he was so charming, the perfect gentleman. Even though he wasn't the most handsome guy, all the girls in my dorm adored him. When he singled me out, I felt like Cinderella at the ball. But the closer we became, the more I was able to see through him. I didn't like what I saw."

"But you stayed together?"

"I tried to break up with him several times," Abby admitted, "but he always managed to get me back. Sometimes he acted like he didn't care, told me no one else would ever love me."

"That's emotional abuse." Scott felt the anger rise inside him at the way Trevor had treated Abby.

"I know." Abby sighed. "But he was so subtle, so convincing. I've often wondered since why he bothered with me. It was almost as though he felt driven to torture someone, and I was the lucky girl. I've never understood why he picked me."

"A lot of guys liked you," Scott informed her matter-of-factly.

Abby blew out a disbelieving shout of air before popping the last of her peanut butter and jelly sandwich into her mouth. After she swallowed, she explained, "Trevor was the only guy who asked me out during my entire four years of college. And you could hardly say I was the prettiest girl there."

"I've always thought you were pretty. In fact, I thought about asking you out, but Trevor beat me to it. Remember how the two of you always walked together to the cafeteria after poetry class?"

Abby rolled her eyes. "Yes."

"Well, one day you were gone from class—"

"I only missed one day," Abby cut in. "That must have been when I had that terrible flu."

"I remember that going around," Scott acknowledged. "That sounds about right. Anyway, Trevor was waiting there for you at the bottom of the steps. I'd been mulling over whether I should ask you out but I didn't know if you were seeing anyone. I figured you were friends with Trevor, so I asked him."

"What did he say?"

"He said the two of you were dating."

For a moment, Abby's face froze. Then her eyebrows knit into a sharp scowl. "But we *weren't* dating. Not when I had the flu. It wasn't until after that…very soon after that."

"So he lied to me." Scott's estimation of Trevor sank even lower. "It figures."

"Scott." Abby squeezed his hand. "I think I know now why Trevor picked me."

Her words sparked realization in his mind. "Because of me?"

"Because if the star quarterback was interested in me, then suddenly I was desirable. He'd been playing the field until then."

With a sinking stomach, Scott realized Abby was probably right. He crunched some trail mix with a disgruntled scowl before chiding himself. "I led him to you. I caused the whole mess he made of your life, all the emotional abuse, everything. I should never have bothered asking Trevor about you. I should have just asked you out."

"I wish you would have."

Her soft words and gentle smile only made Scott feel that much worse for what had happened all those years before. He hated that he'd been a part of Abby's painful past, even if he'd had innocent intentions at the time. And he hated that he'd let her slip past him all those years ago. He *should* have followed his heart and asked her out then. It was a mistake he wouldn't allow himself to repeat. He vowed to ask her out as soon as he had the chance—if he got the chance.

Abby felt like an idiot. As Scott sat silently beside her, his expression intense, maybe even angry, she realized how absurd it was to allow herself to develop feelings for him, much less hint that she'd be open to a relationship. *I wish you would have.* She sounded as though she was begging him to date her!

He probably thought she was one of those angry ex-girlfriends who had nothing better to do than complain about the way the last guy had treated them. She cringed as she recalled the way she'd described Trevor's behavior. Scott was a counselor. He probably got his fill of vindictive women whining during the week. Complaining about her ex was no way to attract Scott to her—not that she had any business trying to attract him.

Deep as her feelings already were for him, his poor mother was missing. She needed to focus on the job ahead and keep her mouth shut. Even if Scott liked her, even a tiny bit, he lived in Minnesota—too far away to develop any sort of ongoing relationship. She would do well to remember that.

"There's Devil's Island." Scott's words pulled her from her thoughts.

She looked up and saw the island, its bright fall leaves eradicated by the previous night's wind, leaving bare skeletal tree branches stabbing morosely at the skyline. Abby hadn't liked the look of Devil's Island the day before. Now the sight of it filled her with cold dread, and she began to silently pray all the more fiercely that God would keep Marilyn safe.

"What's our plan?" she asked aloud, wondering if Scott and Tracie had discussed the next step while they'd been loading supplies.

"I'm not sure, but with all the kayaking equipment we loaded, there's a chance we might be spending some time in the water."

"It's a good day for it," Abby acknowledged, noting the way their wake cut through the otherwise smooth sea. "Just cold."

"Cold isn't so bad as long as we don't get wet."

Abby stifled a giggle, relieved to know they wouldn't be risking as much as they had on their canoe trip the day before. "No kidding."

As the crew docked the boat, Tracie stepped over to talk to them. "Do you two have any ideas about where we should be looking?"

"I thought you were the expert on that," Scott noted.

Tracie shook her head. "We looked everywhere last night, but it was dark and stormy. There's a lot we may have missed. Besides, if Marilyn has only recently been returned to the island, we'll have to recheck everything. I'm sure once all our extra manpower gets here we'll draw up an organized plan, but for now, you might as well just start searching."

"So nobody saw anything last night or this morning?" Abby verified. "Nobody saw any boats arrive?"

Tracie looked remorseful. "We only left a few guys here during the storm. Visibility was next to nothing. Anybody could have come and gone without being seen."

"Then I guess we should just start poking around and see what we can come up with." While she spoke, Abby zippered the last peanut butter and jelly sandwich into one of her coat pockets. She tucked the trail mix into another, silently praying she wouldn't encounter any peanut-loving bears on the island.

"You've got your radios," Tracie confirmed. "You two can split up or stick together, whatever you prefer. Just be sure you contact us immediately if you come across anything suspicious or out of place. We don't have many leads here, so even the smallest thing is worth looking into." Tracie concluded by making sure they each knew how to operate the radios. "Any idea where you might be heading?" she asked once she'd finished their radio tutorial.

Scott turned to Abby. "We never did make it up to the lighthouse yesterday. Why don't we head that way?"

"That sounds like as good a spot as any," Abby agreed.

"Sounds good. We've got men all over the island, with more arriving soon. Just stay in touch," Tracie reminded them as they disembarked.

Abby felt strange walking back up the same trail she and Scott had set out on just over twenty-four hours before. So much had happened since then—more than she wanted to think about. Still, the environmentalist in her was interested to hear more about Scott's plans for conserving his family's land. "So, how long have you and your mother been planning to put your land into easement?"

Scott took a deep breath. "We've talked about it for a long time. It just took a while to get around to it, especially once Mitch came into the picture. He wanted to develop the land, put in a golf course, a water park, you name it."

"A water park?"

"On the lake."

"It has its own lake?"

"It's a pretty big property. Mitch talked my mom into carving up a few acres into lots, so there's a cluster of houses on the north end now, but when he began to move on to the next stage in his development plan, I put my foot down. It was time to put it into easement. That was the plan all along. Before Mitch came along, we'd never used the land for anything other than private hunting, though my grandparents used to harvest maple syrup out there when I was a kid."

"Oh, how neat." Abby had no experience with harvesting maple syrup, but she'd always been intrigued by the idea.

"I always enjoyed it as a kid," Scott acknowledged. "That's been close to twenty years ago, but we spelled out a clause in the easement that would still allow us to run some syrup if we ever wanted to." He paused and looked around.

Abby kept her eyes open, too, for any sign of Marilyn, though she doubted they'd find any in such an obvious place as the trail. Her imagination had been captured by Scott's talk of the conservation easement. She'd worked with many through her job at the Eagle Foundation, and found them to be an ingenious way of protecting natural resources from development while still allowing the original landowners to retain ownership and use of their property. Not only would the land remain protected in perpetuity, but the owners could receive significant tax advantages for their dedication to the public good.

"I love that you're putting the land into easement," Abby encouraged Scott.

He looked down into her face, his eyes glistening with emotion. "I love that you love it."

Abby felt her breath catch, and for a moment she thought he might kiss her again.

But then he simply cleared his throat and continued. "Anyway, the conservation easement was my grandpa's idea. He and my dad did a lot of research on it before he died. The land is at the top of the watershed, and the lake provides excellent habitat. Dad always thought it would be a perfect candidate for easement. In fact, he'd actually started the process right before he died. It's too bad my mom backed off the project once he was gone."

"Didn't she agree with it?"

"I always thought she liked the idea, but she seemed to be so overwhelmed after my father's death. I guess she just didn't have the energy for it."

"I suppose not," Abby said, but her experience with conservation projects told her otherwise. "Still, you'd think she'd want to see it through in his honor." Her mind spun. "Unless Mitch was holding her back. When did you say he came into the picture?"

"They didn't marry until a few months ago, but he'd been wooing her for years. That's where all her diamonds came from—but then, I guess Tim told you that much."

"Wooing her for years," Abby repeated softly as they passed the keeper's quarters and continued up the short path toward the lighthouse.

"You're right," Scott agreed, looking her full in the face and slowing his pace.

"About what?"

"Mitch. The conservation easement. The plot to get my family's land. Mitch didn't just recently fall in with these guys. The diamond smugglers have been planning to take our land all along, haven't they? I should have figured this out before."

Instinctively Abby reached for his arm. "It's okay, Scott. Nobody was openly trying to kill you before. You had no idea anything suspicious was happening. But now that we know, we'll stop them. They won't get away with it." For a moment she looked into his eyes and felt the connection of the shared purpose of their mission.

Then the sound of gunfire rang through the woods.

ELEVEN

Scott covered Abby's head and all but threw her onto his lap as he crouched low on the muddy trail. Abby trembled in his arms like a frightened animal, and Scott realized how close to the surface her fear really was, though she'd acted courageously through all the trials they'd endured so far. The realization only increased his resolve to protect her. When he heard no further shots being fired, he dared to loosen his grip on her and meet her gaze.

She looked terrified. "Are you okay?" she asked.

"I'm fine. It sounded like it was coming from up ahead here."

"Maybe it was one of the Coasties," Abby suggested quickly. "Maybe they found your mother and were taking a shot at her captors."

Scott agreed with her theory. "The gunfire came from up this way." He motioned ahead of them. "Let's hurry, but stay low. We don't know for sure whose side they're on."

They ran, crouched down, to the end of the trail at the northern tip of the island. It wasn't far. The land gave way to open sea in front of them, while the tall white form of the Devil's Island lighthouse spiraled skyward off to their right. "This is the end of the road," Scott pronounced.

Abby stepped off the trail to the left, her face faintly white.

"Is this where…?" Scott began the question, but felt reluctant to voice anything that might be painful to her.

"A little farther over here," Abby explained, quickly making her way sure-footedly through the dense tangle of underbrush on a narrow path so well camouflaged Scott wouldn't have known it was there if he hadn't been walking on it.

They quickly came to a large flat outcropping of brownstone. They looked around the space, but Scott couldn't see any sign that anyone had been in the spot recently. While he poked around, Abby walked closer to the cliffside and peeked out over the edge. Then her face went white and she screamed.

Scott joined her, wrapping one secure arm around her waist lest she fall over the edge in her fright. He peered down over her shoulder and immediately saw what had caused her distress.

A corpse floated facedown in the red-stained water of Lake Superior. Though Scott couldn't be positive who it was, the large frame, dark hair and Coast Guard uniform reminded him for all the world of Trevor Price.

Pulling Abby a few more steps backward, Scott pulled out his radio and contacted the others. "We're out on the north end of the island, about two hundred yards to the west of where the trail ends. There's a body in the lake."

"We heard shots earlier," a voice crackled back in response.

"I'm guessing it's related," Scott acknowledged.

"I'm coming toward you right now." Tracie's voice transmitted over the radio clearly. "I've been headed toward the sound of the gunshots since I heard them. I should be there momentarily."

Scott clipped the radio back into his belt and slung both arms around Abby's shoulders.

She shook him off. "I'm okay. It just surprised me. I've never seen a dead body before—one that wasn't in a coffin. I mean, before Mitch."

Scott winced. He could tell she was trying to be brave, but from her broken sentences and darting eyes he knew she felt extremely shaken. He didn't want to scare her any further, but at the same time, he felt she needed to know the identity of the victim. "Abby, I don't know if you recognized—"

"It's Trevor," she said bluntly, and met his eyes. "I may not have spent much time around him in several years, but I still recognize him from the back."

Scott pulled her back into his arms and stood close to a large tree. "He may have been standing right on this ledge when he was shot. The shooter could still be in the vicinity," he explained.

They heard rustling in the woods.

Scott could feel Abby tense in his arms. He crouched lower and leaned hard against the tree, shielding Abby with his body, though if it came to a battle between the wind-warped wood and a bullet, he doubted the hemlock would offer them much protection.

"There you are," Tracie's voice called out to them. "And the body?"

"Over the ledge." Scott sighed with relief when he recognized the Coastie, though he immediately feared what her reaction might be when she saw her fallen partner. He had no idea how close she'd been to Trevor, but even if they hadn't been great friends, the sight of her fallen comrade would surely shake her.

Sure enough, Tracie let out a gasp, then looked at the two of them with wide eyes. "It's Trevor."

Scott nodded. "We thought so."

Tracie's jaw clenched. She pulled out her radio and spat out instructions in a combination of English and various codes. Scott heard her describe the victim—white male, six foot five, bullet wounds in the back—but he noted she never used his name. It was probably best that way. They didn't know who might be listening in.

She put her radio away and looked at the two of them. "Let's get back to the boat. We're going to need those kayaks to retrieve the body."

They hurried back toward the trail in silence. Scott didn't figure the shooter would stick around, but he didn't want to do anything to draw attention to himself, either. They hadn't gone far before they met a team of Coast Guardsmen on the trail.

Scott recognized them from the evening before—John and Mack, two of the guys who'd stayed the night on the island. They looked a little tired under the eyes, but alert.

"Headed back?" John asked.

Tracie nodded. "We're going to get the boat and bring it around. I don't know how else to retrieve the body."

Mack patted his backpack. "I've got rope. We might be able to rappel down and pull it up after us."

"I doubt it, but you can try." Tracie shrugged. "We'll hurry with the boat."

"Sure thing." John looked warily down the trail. "Any idea if the gunman is still in the area?"

"We're still alive," Tracie pointed out.

Mack chuckled. "Any clue to the identity of the victim?"

"It's Trevor."

Mack sobered. *"Trevor Price?"*

"But he's supposed to be on leave after last night's…incident." John looked uneasily at Scott, then back to Tracie. "He shouldn't have even been out here."

"Well, he was, and he was in uniform."

John shook his head and muttered a few unkind words about the deceased's lack of judgment.

Tracie ignored his comments. "We're going to hurry with that boat." She repeated instructions on where to find the body and then led Scott and Abby back down the hill.

The encounter with Mack and John had broken the spell of silence.

"Well, now we know why we couldn't find him last night. How did you two discover the body?" Tracie asked as they hustled down the road.

"I looked out over the edge, and there it was," Abby answered in a hollow voice.

Tracie sounded intrigued. "What led you to that spot? I never knew that ledge was there. You must not have wasted much time since we split up. It's only been a matter of minutes since the shots were fired. Did you see any sign of anyone?"

"No," Abby answered.

"Then how did you know where to look?"

"We heard the shots fired," Scott started to explain.

Abby put a hand on his arm and mouthed the words, *It's okay.* Then she cleared her throat and explained, "About six years ago, I spent the summer stationed out here when I was working for the Park Service. Trevor and I were sort of dating at the time and, well, he proposed to me right there on that ledge."

Tracie's pace slowed until the three of them walked

evenly together. "He proposed to you in the same spot where he was shot? That's a little weird, don't you think?"

"Yeah," Abby acknowledged, her face pale. "I thought about that already. I wonder if it's more than a coincidence."

"Nothing else that's happened this weekend has been 'just a coincidence,'" Scott volunteered. He'd had his own concerns about the unlikely correlation.

"Was it a favorite spot of his?" Tracie asked. "Did he go there often?"

"Not to my knowledge. I'd never been to that spot before he proposed to me."

Scott reached for Abby's hand and squeezed it. "Can you tell us about the proposal? How did it happen?"

Abby let out a shaky breath.

"Please?" Scott prodded. "I know it can't be easy thinking about it, especially with Trevor—" He caught himself and cleared his throat. "I know it can't be easy," he repeated, "but it might give us a clue. You helped me look back on the painful events of my life, and if it hadn't been for that, we might still have no idea why my mother was taken. Maybe your memories can help us find her. Please?"

Abby pinched her eyes shut tightly. She could still see Trevor's body floating facedown in the cold Gitche-Gumee, could still see the dark red welts in his left shoulder and the blood wafting from them as the waves sloshed over him. She didn't want to think any more about him. But Scott had an excellent point. And besides, she didn't want him to think she was still stewing over an old beau.

"It was the end of the summer tourist season. We were going to lock up the keeper's quarters in a couple of days. Already traffic to the island had slowed down considerably. Trevor was working for the Park Service, too, then. He was stationed on Rocky, but he came over to visit me quite a bit. One evening he called and said he wanted to come over. I cooked supper, but then he disappeared while I was cleaning up. That wasn't unusual. He only washed dishes if he was trying to be extra-nice to gain something."

"That sounds like Trevor," Tracie chimed in.

Abby managed a faint smile. "I had seen him head up the trail toward the end of the island, so I went walking up that way. It was a beautiful evening, one of those late summer days when it's not even cold out here. The water was gentle, and it was getting close to sunset."

As Abby closed her eyes and tried to remember the long-suppressed details, their radios buzzed.

"Uh, Tracie? Mack here."

Tracie responded to Mack, and he continued.

"We found the spot, and I'll grant you, maybe the water does look a little reddish down there, but we can't see a body anywhere."

John's voice carried over the radio. "And Trevor was a big guy, so it's not like he'd be easy to hide."

Tracie rolled her eyes. "The waves probably washed him under the rim of the bluffs or into a sea cave or something. We'll check it out when we get over there with the boat."

"Fine. You want us to stick around?"

"No. Search and Rescue takes precedence over body retrieval. Just keep your eyes open for that gunman, and let me know if you come across anything suspicious."

The guys signaled that they'd received her message.

Abby took a deep breath. "Maybe we should just hurry to the boat. I can tell my story another time."

"No." Tracie shook her head. "Your story is important. We'll hurry to the boat, but please keep talking."

They trotted a few more yards and Abby continued. "So, where was I? I went walking down the trail, but when I got to the sea cliffs Trevor wasn't there. I figured I must have missed him. Then I thought I heard voices."

"You *thought* you heard voices?" Tracie clarified.

"It wasn't very loud, nothing distinct. And obviously it wasn't voices unless Trevor was talking to himself, because I stumbled upon that little rabbit run and followed it until I found him. He was alone."

Abby focused on her feet as they hurried down the road, avoiding any slick patches on the frozen clay. "He didn't really look all that happy to see me, at first glance. It was funny, because my initial impression was that I'd interrupted him or something. He sometimes had a temper, so you never wanted to make him mad. But maybe I just got there before he was quite ready, or something. I started to ask him who he was talking to and the next thing I knew, he ran over to me, picked me up and gave me this big kiss. He swung me around in circles, and when he set me down, he pulled a diamond ring out of his pocket and proposed. Right there, just like that."

They hustled down the road in silence for a few moments. Then Scott asked, "So, do you think he was planning on proposing to you right then? He had the ring and everything, but that's strange that he didn't ask you to come out and meet him."

"You know," Abby confessed, "I always thought it was a little odd. We hadn't even been getting along very well at that point. We weren't even technically dating, but he'd called me up and invited himself over for supper."

"That sounds like Trevor," Tracie chimed in.

Abby almost smiled as she continued. "And, well, it might sound silly, but I never felt the ring was the right choice for me."

"Why not?" Scott asked.

"I'd always said I wanted my engagement ring to match my eyes. That's foolish, I suppose, but I *know* I'd told Trevor that before. It seemed strange that he'd disregard it, like he either didn't remember or didn't care. I guess I just…" Abby paused. She wasn't sure she wanted to share the next bit. "I felt it was odd, the whole proposal thing. It came out of the blue, and there was a moment, right after I told him yes, when Trevor looked almost…annoyed." She shook her head. "But then, I suppose, if he was already working for the diamond smugglers…"

They'd come out of the woods while Abby spoke, and now Tracie patted her shoulder. "Thank you for sharing that. It does seem odd, and it makes me wonder if there wasn't more going on than we understand. We'll talk about it, but right now, let's get on the boat and hurry around to the other side of the island."

The three of them hopped back into the utility boat and Tracie rushed to start the engine. Then she turned to Scott and Abby. "If we're going to use the kayaks in this weather, you two need wet suits, neoprene and Gore-Tex. There should be plenty of waterproof garments in the bags we loaded. Scott, can you help Abby find something that fits?"

After they rustled up the proper cold-weather gear, Scott and Abby ducked into separate rooms in the boat's small cabin. Then Scott took over the wheel while Tracie changed. By the time the boat reached the northern tip of the island, the three of them were snugly dressed for cold-weather kayaking.

Tracie idled the motor, slowly trolling closer to the land and the few rocky outcroppings that extended beyond the sea caves. "I don't see any sign of Trevor," she murmured, her eyes scanning the rocky formations.

"There's the lighthouse." Scott pointed. "We'd gone about two hundred yards southwest, so that puts us right about here." He gestured to a spot just beyond them.

Once Tracie killed the motor, the lapping of the relatively still waters did little to disturb the eerie silence. Abby stared at the sea caves, wondering how a boat of any size, much less a pirate ship, could have fit into any of them. The rocks were dangerous for any craft, especially in rough weather. Then she noticed a particularly large opening, and beside it, like lamb's blood on a lintel, a splash of red.

"Look at that, just beyond that large cave mouth." Abby indicated the spot. "Is that what I think it is?"

Tracie pulled out a camera and zoomed in on the spot. "Blood." She snapped several photos.

"Trevor's blood?" Scott asked aloud.

"Probably." Tracie took a deep breath and put away her camera. "But if so, then he wasn't standing on that ledge up there when he was shot. He would have been standing there." She pointed to a low rocky outcropping that extended back toward the wide opening and the fresh bloodstain. "And he would have been shot from this direction, which would have meant a boat, at sea." Skepticism showed on her face. "You didn't see a boat?"

Abby's mouth fell open, and she looked around her at the open sea. There was no sign of any vessel anywhere.

"No, I didn't. I mean, I was pretty distracted by the dead body, but I can't imagine missing seeing something as big as a boat. But then, you reached the ledge barely a minute later. Did you see anything?"

The skeptical expression fled from Tracie's features. "No, I didn't. Good point. Maybe it wasn't a boat. Maybe it was just a kayak, and they slipped away into the caves."

At the mention of the sea caves, all three of them peered at the wide dark opening, whose inky blackness could have concealed anyone, or anything…including the gunman. Abby felt a shiver run up her spine, and she had to fight off the instinct to duck. She nearly jumped when Scott wrapped one arm around her.

"It's okay," he whispered, obviously having felt her jolt of surprise. "It's just me."

While they stood blinking in incomprehension at the empty water, Tracie shoved supplies into the pockets of her parka, snapped on neoprene gloves and then grabbed a kayak and carried it to the edge of the boat. "I'm going to get a sample of that blood. Then I'm going into the cave. Are you two coming with me?"

Abby nodded. There was something in that cave. There had to be. Marilyn could be in there. Or Trevor's body. Or the gunman, waiting for them.

TWELVE

Though Scott had no experience launching kayaks, with Abby's help they managed to get their vessels into the lake without taking on water. At Tracie's instruction, they anchored the utility boat before slipping into their kayaks. By that time, Tracie had collected a sample from the blood on the brownstone and was ready to join them exploring the sea caves.

Scott was glad for the headlamps mounted on each kayak, as well as the LED lights they each wore on a headband. But as they paddled the short distance to the gaping maw of the sea cave, he realized the powerful lights were feeble weapons against the pressing darkness. Shadows loomed in every corner, spilling out at odd angles as their lights drifted by, taunting them with the possibility of what could be hidden under the cloak of their darkness.

Their crafts glided silently into the cave. Scott tried to maneuver his kayak so his light would pan across the back wall of the cave. As Abby had previously predicted, the cave ended a mere sixty or seventy feet from the spot where it opened to the sea. There was enough space to shelter a decent-size boat, yes, but the wide mouth of the cave offered no cover. The pirates in Burt's story wouldn't have lasted long hiding from the authorities in this wide-open space, and neither would the diamond smugglers. Any vessel sailing past the north side of the island would have seen them easily if they'd attempted to hide there.

"I'm not seeing a body anywhere," Tracie murmured, her words echoing against the brownstone walls and resonating dissonantly with the sounds of the lapping waves.

"What if he sank?" Scott suggested, looking down into the clear water. "I wonder how deep the water is here." Holding tight to one end of his paddle, he plunged the other end downward…and never felt bottom. As the force of the lapping water pressed against his paddle, it almost felt as though the lake was trying to pull it from his hands. He quickly pulled the paddle back up. "It's at least six feet deep, and could be infinitely deeper," he speculated.

"Deep enough to hide a body," Abby agreed. "But Trevor was pretty buoyant."

Scott smiled at the polite way Abby referred to her ex-fiancé's extra girth. "What if he was weighed down by something? He could have been carrying heavy equipment in his pockets or on his person."

Tracie pointed out, "If he'd have been wearing a bullet-proof vest, it might have been heavy enough to pull him under. But that's why we Coasties rarely wear the vests, even though we have a crime-fighting role out here. The odds of ending up in the lake are much higher than the odds of being shot." She paddled closer to the ledge that extended along one back corner of the cave. "And anyway, if he'd have been wearing a vest, there wouldn't have been blood, and he probably wouldn't have died."

"Good point," Scott noted, but Tracie didn't appear to

be listening anymore. She was staring intently at something on the ledge.

"What do you suppose?" she mused aloud, then pulled out her camera and snapped a few more pictures before panning her light farther along the wall. "Could one of you come hold my kayak?" she asked a moment later.

Scott paddled over and held her craft steady while she climbed out onto the brownstone. He watched as she dabbed gauze at something smeared on the ledge, and then placed it in a plastic bag from her pocket. It wasn't until she pulled out a marker and labeled the bag that Scott was sure what she'd swabbed up from the ledge.

Blood—inside cave.

"Trevor's blood?" Scott asked quietly.

Tracie shrugged and stuffed the baggie into her pocket. "It appears to be fresh, just like the spatter outside."

Abby had paddled over near them and was watching with interest. "But what would his blood be doing way back in here? It isn't as though he'd have likely drifted up onto the ledge, and his body clearly isn't here anymore."

Though they'd nearly ruled out the possibility already, Scott flashed his light downward into the deep clear waters below them. The pool appeared to have no bottom. From his vantage point close to the edge, Scott could see the brownstone drop away sharply, disappearing into the watery abyss below. It was a chilling sight, but there was still no sign of a body.

"If he was shot from a boat or a kayak," Tracie pondered aloud, "and then whoever shot him hid inside this cave, they probably heard us talking up above and decided to dispose of the evidence before we could recover anything incriminating."

Scott looked around warily, half expecting the gunman to suddenly appear in the mouth of the cave behind him. The hairs on his arms and neck stood on end.

"But why would they pull the body onto the ledge?" Abby pressed.

"Perhaps they heard John and Mack coming and got spooked. Or, I don't know, maybe they wanted to search him. Maybe they thought he had something on him, something they wanted."

Cautiously, Scott paddled back the way they'd come, back into the daylight that made him squint with its sudden brightness. He stared at the low rock where Trevor had apparently been standing when he'd been shot. Then his eyes traveled farther back to where the shallow rocks cupped a still pool of water before giving way to the brownstone cliffs that rose upward to meet the sun.

On a hunch, Scott beached his kayak on the small rocky spit where Tracie had left hers when she'd collected the sample earlier. But instead of inspecting the spatter, he stepped past it to the shallow pool that was protected from the action of the waves by the outcropping. There he crouched down, his eyes scanning the rock, until something caught his eye. He squinted, leaning closer for a better look, nearly missing the gray object hidden among the darker rocks.

He shouted to the women, "Come take a look at this."

Abby arrived first, and he plucked up the ring, holding it out to her almost reverently. "Do you recognize this?"

"Yes." She met his eyes.

"I was a groomsman at my mother's second wedding. I still vividly remember Mitch showing this off to the guys before the wedding, boasting about what it was worth. I haven't paid much attention to it since then, but I thought it looked familiar."

As he spoke, Tracie paddled around the rock. "What's that?" she asked.

"Mitch's wedding ring. I found it right here." He tapped the spot with his foot, and the shallow water splashed.

"So Trevor still had the ring," Abby muttered. "Whoever killed him must have figured he had it on him. They probably took his body in order to get the ring."

Scott looked at her and suddenly realized how difficult the situation must be, finding a wedding ring so close to the spot where the recently deceased had once proposed to her. But she seemed to be holding herself together just fine. "Do you think it may have been the same people who told him to get your ring back from you?" he asked her quietly.

"I'd say almost certainly," Abby agreed. "The two have got to be related."

"Wait." Tracie steered her kayak around until she faced them both. "What are you guys talking about? Are what two related? Do you know something I don't know? Because if so, *now* is the time to tell me."

"Remember how I told you earlier that Trevor proposed to me on that ledge?" Abby pointed upward. "Well, he showed up at my place a couple of nights ago and demanded I return the ring to him."

"Did you?"

"Not yet." Abby's hand went around to the backside of her two-piece wetsuit. "In fact, I have it on me right now." She pulled out a handful of diamond jewelry. "And Marilyn's earrings, which I'll hand over as evidence because I have no more use for them than I do for the ring. I'm not a jewelry person, but all of a sudden there seems to be a lot of diamond jewelry in my life. But apparently they aren't even real."

Tracie paddled her kayak closer and gingerly accepted the jewels from Abby. She zippered them securely into a plastic bag and labeled it. Scott made sure she got Mitch's ring in with the others before she tucked them into an interior pocket of her jacket.

Scott climbed back into his kayak. "Let's not let ourselves get too distracted from our mission here," he reminded them. "We came down here to retrieve a body. Right now we still have no idea where that body went."

Abby settled back into the seat of her kayak as well. "None of us saw a boat, and there's too much wide-open lake for them to have gotten in and out without us spotting them."

"It seems to me, after we saw the body floating here, somebody dragged it onto that ledge inside the sea cave. But where did they take it from there?" As Scott talked, he paddled back into the deep darkness of the sea cave. The place still made him nervous, but the slow pace of their search was starting to irk him. His mother was still missing, and now so was Trevor's body. They were getting further behind instead of closer to their goal.

The women paddled up next to him as he shined his light on the still-visible smear of blood on the ledge.

"Someone pulled the body onto that ledge. But from there, where could they possibly have gone?"

"Perhaps they tied weights to him and sank him," Abby suggested.

Scott looked back down into the depths of the water and could see nothing but bottomless darkness. "I suppose that's possible."

"Or," Abby continued, "what about the back wall?"

She shined her light back. "The ledge continues on for some distance."

"Yes," Tracie acknowledged, "but it gets narrower back there, not wider. And those walls are smooth. There's not the slightest nook or cranny where you could hide a little guy, let alone someone the size of Trevor."

Despite Tracie's words of doubt, Scott wondered if Abby might be onto something. "Hold my kayak," he requested, then scrambled up onto the ledge, taking care not to disturb the bloodstain. He carefully made his way along the stone shelf, his eyes searching, his mind replaying the moment when he'd spotted the ring in the pool, as though at any instant he might happen upon another important clue.

"Shine some more light over here, could you?" he requested, squatting down to inspect a spot near his feet. As Tracie angled her headlight his way, Scott nodded. "Blood. They must have carried the body this way."

"They? Carried?" Tracie repeated. "Did I mention that Trevor was a big guy?"

Scott dismissed her doubts. The evidence before his eyes meant more to him than her words. He crept farther along, bracing himself against the wall until his hand touched something moist. He looked at his palm. "More blood."

"The body must have rubbed against the wall of the cave," Abby theorized as she floated her kayak toward him.

A moment later, Scott came to the end of the ledge. He felt a brief disappointment as he stared at the smooth back wall of the cave.

Then he realized it wasn't entirely smooth.

A crack ran through the stone—a remarkably straight crack that didn't look the same as the natural breaks and fissures he'd seen elsewhere in the rock. A smear of blood streaked the stone along part of the seam—a smear of blood in the shape of a handprint.

"Ladies, come look at this," Scott requested.

Tracie paddled over with her camera and zoomed in on the spot, taking picture after picture. Abby climbed up beside him on the ledge and clutched his arm as she peered over his shoulder. Her warm presence helped ease the fear he'd been feeling.

"What is that?" Abby spoke in an awed whisper, her breath warming his ear.

Scott could see a slight indentation in the seam beneath the bloody handprint. He turned to Tracie. "Mind if I touch it?"

"I have my pictures." She nodded. "Go ahead, but try not to disturb it any more than necessary."

Scott fitted his fingers into the depression. As he probed the seam, the rock shifted, allowing him to slide his hand back into the rock. A section of stone eased away from the cliff wall, and Scott tugged on it a little more sharply. Then he heard the sound of rushing water.

"What's that?" Abby asked.

They looked. Across the back of the cave, water shot like a high-powered waterfall from an opening in the rock. And then, as they watched, the entire back wall of the cave began to rise.

Abby clung to Scott's arm in fear and amazement. The sound of rushing water and a distant ratcheting boom filled the small cave, making conversation impossible, even if Abby would have been able to think of something to say. She felt as though she'd stepped into a dream, as though reality had given way before her eyes just as the rear wall of the cave was disappearing.

Water sluiced through channels cut behind the rock, and thick, rusty chains clanged past them, their heavy counterweights obeying the course that appeared to be set in motion when Scott had tugged on the trigger mechanism. The whole thing seemed little more complicated than a garage door, though it was camouflaged with real rock and apparently constructed over a century before.

As the cave wall rose, Abby quickly realized the space behind it was illuminated from somewhere within. At the same moment, it occurred to her that the three of them had no idea what they were getting into. They'd clearly found the century-old pirates hideout. But just as clearly, someone else had found it long before them.

"Let's get out of here," she hissed into Scott's ear.

His grip tightened on her arm, and he turned back toward her. "You're right. We need to get backup."

In the water, Tracie turned her kayak around.

But before any of them could go anywhere, a voice called out, "You can just stop right there."

Abby looked toward the source of the voice. The wall continued to rise, revealing more of the space hidden under the island. Water filled half of a vast room larger than a full city block. The other half of the cavern was some sort of pier, where boxes and crates were stacked in rows extending back against the brownstone walls. Though several banks of lights hung from iron catwalks crisscrossing the ceiling, only the rear lights were turned on, their greenish glow illuminating a network of desks and computers. Even from a distance, they provided enough light for Abby to make out much of the interior of the cave.

A good-size yacht was docked along the pier that ran the length of the cavern. And beside it, closest to the cave opening, the *Helene* bobbed innocently in the water. Captain Sal stood on her deck with a gun in his hand.

"You three come easy and I won't have to shoot," he called.

Abby didn't even consider trying to run for it. She stepped across the threshold with Scott as the ledge gave way to a wide-open platform and finally a pier made of metal and wood.

Six thugs approached them as they entered. Two pulled Tracie roughly from her kayak, and the others quickly bound their wrists behind their backs with lengths of fabric. Hands wrenched away their headlamps, radios and Tracie's camera and sidearm.

The Coastie scowled at them.

"Careful now, boys," Captain Sal cautioned. "We don't want any marks on the bodies. No signs of violence, nothing to indicate foul play. These three are going to die in an unfortunate accident, just like Marilyn Adams."

At the mention of his mother's name, Abby felt Scott stiffen beside her. But before either of them had a chance to respond, they were pushed through the darkness down the pier. Abby looked all around her, trying to take in as many details as possible. If she ever got the chance, she wanted to be able to explain clearly what she'd seen in that unknown space.

Rough hands steered her and the others toward a large metal door. From the looks of it, Abby guessed it dated back all the way to the time of the pirates a century before, or possibly longer back than that. But the thick chains and padlocks on the outside were definitely newer and looked impenetrable. Two different men took out keys, unlocking the securely fastened door before shoving the three of them inside.

A slice of light pierced the empty room. Then the door shuddered shut behind them and they were left in utter darkness.

THIRTEEN

Abby leaned against Scott. His arms were bound behind him, but she felt him leaning counterweight against her, supporting her even as she supported him.

A weak voice cut through the gloom. "Scott? Honey, is that you?"

Shuffling noises sounded from the far corner of the room. Scott straightened beside her. "Mom?"

"Oh, Scott, honey!"

Abby could see nothing, but she heard Marilyn coming closer, and then felt the impact of her body as she rushed to her son.

"Mom! Are you okay? Are you hurt?"

"I'm okay. I finally got those ropes off. Here, let me untie you."

Scott continued to pepper his mother with questions. "How did you get here? How long have you been here?"

As Marilyn tugged at the fabric that bound her son, she explained, "Captain Sal came back last night. A storm had started to blow up, and I was nervous about what had become of you and Abby, and then out of nowhere, here comes the *Helene.* I had a horrible feeling something was up, but Mitch seemed to think Captain Sal had just gotten his times mixed up after all. He told me to get on the boat. I shouldn't have listened, but with the weather getting bad, I thought I couldn't possibly be worse off on the boat than standing out in the storm." She shook her head, finally tugging Scott free with a grunt.

Scott gave his mother a long hug before he turned his attention to untying Abby.

"Are you sure we should untie ourselves? Won't that make them angry?" Abby asked, concerned. She'd seen enough people shot—she knew Captain Sal's threats weren't empty.

"Oh, probably," Marilyn chided, "but they're angry enough as it is. They'll just tie us up again anyway. In the meantime, it's no fun stumbling around in the dark when you don't have use of your hands." Marilyn looked at Tracie warily. "Who's this? Do we want to untie her?"

Scott explained Tracie's role in the investigation. Abby noticed that he left out anything having to do with Mitch. She recalled his earlier insistence on avoiding upsetting his mother, and figured it was for the best, at this point.

While Scott tugged on the tight knot behind her, Abby's eyes began to adjust to the darkness. She realized there was a very faint beam of light coming down through the solid rock of the ceiling—probably one of the natural fissures in the stone, much like the blowholes they'd witnessed aboveground. Though it stretched three feet long or more, it couldn't have been more than eight inches wide at the broadest point.

Then Scott had her hands free and his arms back around his mother. For several minutes mother and son simply held each other. "You're sure you're okay?" he asked again.

"Just hungry, and more than a little spooked," Marilyn confessed. "But they've been very careful not to injure me. Captain Sal insisted on that."

At the mention of food, Abby dug through her pockets and pulled out the last peanut butter and jelly sandwich and the remains of the trail mix they'd shared on the boat ride over. Fortunately the thugs hadn't confiscated them. "Here, Marilyn." She pressed the food into her hands. "Do you like PB&J?"

"Love it," Marilyn exclaimed. "But even if I didn't, I'd eat it. You're sure you don't want to save this?"

"No, I've had my fill. Please," Abby insisted. In the back of her mind, she wondered if she'd live to see another meal. Not if Captain Sal got his way. She pushed the thought away.

Marilyn made quick work of the sandwich, between bites questioning them about what had happened to them since they'd rowed away in the canoe the day before. Scott began the story, but before he reached the part with Mitch's involvement, Tracie stopped him.

"I hate to interrupt, but those guys out there intend to kill us, and I don't intend to die."

Though she agreed, Abby couldn't imagine what they could possibly do about it. "Yes. What do you think we should do?"

Tracie pointed to the crack in the ceiling. "I want to go for help."

Abby looked at the narrow fissure and then looked at Tracie. Granted, the other woman was uncommonly slender. She'd have a better shot than Abby of fitting through the tiny space. "But that's got to be fifteen feet high," Abby protested. "We have no way of getting you up there." She looked around the room, although as she'd already concluded, it was completely empty.

"Good idea," Marilyn agreed. "What am I doing standing around eating? We've got to get you out of here."

"But do you really think—" Abby began to protest when she felt Scott's hand on her shoulder and he whispered in her ear. "Floss."

Then he spoke in a louder, cheery voice, "Is there anything around here we could use to climb up there?"

It took a moment for Abby to figure out what Scott had meant by his ambiguous reference, especially since she didn't have any more floss with her, and had left her purse on the utility boat. Then she recalled the discussion they'd had the day before about giving his mother a project to work on to keep her from becoming overly anxious. Though she feared their efforts would be futile, Abby realized doing *something* would be better than doing nothing, even if it didn't get them anywhere.

"Well, son," Marilyn began, "I've been in this little room for all of today and most of last night. The back and side walls are solid rock, and the front is cement around the door. I think I've explored every inch of it, and I can tell you there wasn't a thing in here, not a loose rock, not a sparc rope, not anything before you three arrived. But now that you're here, we finally have something we can work with."

"What's that?" Scott asked, clearly as bewildered as Abby felt.

"Us!"

While Abby stared at her, dumbfounded, Marilyn explained her plan to make a human chain extending up toward the skylight. Though she felt skeptical their efforts would achieve anything more than bumps and bruises, and maybe broken limbs or concussions, when she recalled Captain Sal's insistence that they not be injured, she smiled to herself. Yes, Marilyn's plan sounded pretty crazy, but if injury was the worst that could happen, Abby was all for it.

"Okay," she agreed. "Let's do it."

They agreed that if Abby stood on Scott's shoulders, and Tracie stood on Abby's shoulders, they should have enough height between the three of them to reach the gap in the ceiling. Fortunately, the fissure was close to the back wall of the cave. As Scott pointed out, he and Abby had successfully managed a similar human chain the day before at the shed. Adding one more person couldn't be that difficult—could it?

Abby told herself it didn't so much matter whether their plan was really as ridiculous as it sounded. They needed to do *something,* and she didn't have any better suggestions. Besides, there was still some slim chance the crazy scheme could work. She'd seen more outrageous stunts at the circus.

Though Abby had taken several strength training classes at the Bayfield Recreation Center over the years, she wasn't sure how well she'd manage supporting Tracie's slight weight for any amount of time. Still she crouched down and allowed the other woman to step up onto her shoulders. With Tracie clutching at the rough wall for balance and Abby pushing against her knees as she stood, Scott hovered close behind, lending balance and a little extra lift. Slowly, Abby stood.

The tricky part, then, was for Abby to step up onto Scott's shoulders so he could stand with the two of them wobbling ten feet above his head. They made several

attempts. Most ended with Tracie sliding down the length
of the wall, but when she fell backward and landed with a
thump, Abby stretched her overworked leg muscles with
a sigh. "I don't think this is working."

"No, I'm okay," Tracie insisted. "We can do this. Let's
give it another go."

But this time, Marilyn sided with Abby. "Let's take a
break."

"But Captain Sal and his men could come back for us
any moment," Scott protested. "We don't have much time."

Marilyn gave her son a stern look. "We need to pray."

"She's right," Abby agreed immediately. "Let's pray."
She looked at Tracie uncertainly. "Are you okay with that?"

"Of course." Tracie nodded. "We should have thought
of it sooner."

The four of them joined hands and Marilyn immediately
began by thanking God for protecting them and bringing
them back together. Then Scott asked for wisdom in how
to proceed, and Tracie requested strength.

As soon as Tracie's prayer concluded, Abby began,
"And, Lord, we know Your word says that You're with us."
Her voice cracked. "The darkness isn't dark to You, and no
obstacle is too big for You. So we ask You to help us see
what we need to do, and give us strength to do it. Amen."

The other three joined her with the *Amen,* and Scott
squeezed her hand. Abby felt lighter somehow, as though
a great burden had been lifted.

Tracie clapped her hands together. "Let's do this."

Having practiced the move several times before, Abby
squatted down and held tight to Tracie's ankles as the other
woman stepped onto her shoulders. But having lifted
Tracie's weight so many times already, Abby's leg muscles

protested painfully as she rose. She focused on breathing steadily in through her nose and out through her mouth. God would give her the strength to stand.

Once Abby stood straight, Tracie's weight was easier to bear locked into place by her upright posture.

"Okay." Scott spoke softly close to her ear as he stood with his solid arms supporting her. "I'm going to have you sit you on my shoulders and then lift you to a standing position. You don't have to bend your legs."

"But that's not how we did it before."

"I know. That's why it's going to work this time."

"But it's too much weight for you to bear," Abby protested.

"You've been taking on more than your fair share," Scott insisted as he ducked down and grasped her knees. "Let's just try this."

"Okay," Abby agreed shakily. She reminded herself that they'd prayed—perhaps Scott's new approach was a gift from God. As he slowly stood, with Abby sitting piggyback on his shoulders and Tracie standing balanced on Abby's shoulders, Abby realized how much easier it was on her to let Scott do all the lifting. She recalled his earlier penchant for carrying the burdens of others, but this time she was glad for it. She honestly didn't know how much more standing and lifting she could take.

"Now I'm going to lift you up," Scott explained once he stood upright.

"What do you want me to do?" Abby asked.

"Nothing. Just try not to lose your balance. Use the wall as much as you can to stabilize yourself."

It was easier said than done. As Scott began to lift her by the seat of her pants, she was glad for the rubberized wet suit that allowed him to grasp her easily. More so, she appreciated his massive upper body strength as he hoisted the weight of both women above his head.

After a moment's grunting struggle, she managed to perch on his shoulders on her knees. She could hear him panting as he caught his breath beneath her.

"I can reach the ceiling now," Tracie called down. "I think we can do this."

Abby wasn't so sure, but she refused to voice her doubts. Everyone was giving it their all. She wasn't about to deter them.

"Do you want me to try to stand?" she asked Scott in a shaky voice. She could feel the strain on her leg muscles again, and her back felt as though it would crumple under the constant weight of the woman on her shoulders.

"Yeah," Scott conceded. "I guess you're going to have to. I'll give you all the lift I can add from down here, but you're getting too high up for me to do much more."

Cautiously, Abby proceeded to move upward. Now that Tracie held firm to the ceiling, anchoring them, it was easier to balance, which helped with the strain on her leg muscles. Still, she wobbled horribly before she finally had both of her feet solidly on Scott's shoulders. She let out an exhausted breath. "We're up," she announced.

"Okay, now I'm going to move us closer to the opening."

Abby was reluctant to lose her contact with the wall of the cave, but they were still a foot or two from the fissure on the ceiling. She pulled her hands up to her shoulders and held tight to Tracie's ankles, steadying her as she crouched just below the top of the cave.

"Got it," Tracie called, and Abby could feel her straighten up inside the space. "I fit. I can reach." She paused. "I can *almost* reach the top."

"Can you pull yourself up?" Scott's voice sounded strained.

"It's too slick. The sides are rock and clay, and it's damp. There's nothing to hold on to. I just need a few more inches. I can feel the edge of the hole, but I can't get enough leverage with my hands."

It wasn't until Abby realized they wouldn't be able to make it after all that she recognized she'd begun to hope their outrageous plan would work.

But then a voice spoke from below.

"Scott, stand on my back." Marilyn lay down on the floor.

"Mother, no," Scott protested. "We're too heavy. It will hurt you."

"Son—" Marilyn's voice took on a no-nonsense mothering tone "—I said step on my back. You either risk hurting me, or we all die."

Abby could feel the hesitation in Scott's trembling muscles as his body moved slightly forward…and then up. Though she didn't dare look down from her dizzying height, she could imagine Marilyn lying on the floor below them, and hated to think how much weight the older woman had taken on.

No sooner did she think about the weight, than she felt the burden on her shoulders ease. Instinctively she lifted up on Tracie's ankles.

"I'm up! I'm through!" the other woman called down, and with a thrashing kick of her legs, Tracie disappeared up through the hole.

With nothing more to anchor her to the ceiling, Abby lost her perch on Scott's shoulders. She felt him jump down from his mother's back and an instant later, displaying all the dexterity of the quarterback he'd once been, he caught Abby as she fell.

Scott pulled Abby into his arms and didn't let go. "Thank you," he whispered when he could finally talk.

"Thank you," she countered. "And thank you to your mother. Marilyn, how are you?"

"Well, my chiropractor's going to have a fit when he sees me, but I think I'll live." She gave them both a meaningful look, her face caught in the dim light from the fissure. "I think we'll all live."

"Let's just pray Tracie reaches help in time," Abby noted.

"You're right," Scott agreed, impressed that she'd made the suggestion, and equally pleased that she'd prayed aloud with them earlier. "We should pray. That's how Paul and Silas got out of prison in the book of Acts."

Marilyn spoke up. "I think that's an excellent idea, but I believe there's one thing we ought to do first."

"What's that?"

"Let's tie up our wrists again. If we tie the knots ourselves, we can use slipknots so we'll be able to easily undo them when we need to. But if we wait for those thugs to tie us up, we won't be able to break free very easily."

"Mom's right," Scott agreed. He found the lengths of fabric where they'd dropped them on the floor. "We don't know when those guys are coming back for us, so we should hurry up and do this now."

The first two knots were easy enough to tie, but when it came to Marilyn's turn to be bound, Scott and Abby had to work together, standing backward, to secure her wrists behind her.

"There." Scott sighed and took a step back. "That should hold. It's not pretty, so try not to let them see it."

"Agreed." Marilyn nodded and sat down on the damp muddy floor. "Now let's pray."

They found the most comfortable way to sit was with their backs together in a circle, supporting each other's weight. Scott's legs and shoulders were exhausted, and he felt particularly sore in the places that had been overworked the day before. He knew Abby had to feel just as miserable, but she didn't complain. He felt appreciation swell inside his heart. He'd sensed she hadn't wanted to try the human ladder, but she'd given it her all. If they lived, he'd owe her for his life once again.

Once they were all situated, they began to pray, first that Tracie would reach help and then that help would reach them in time. They prayed for strength and guidance. The only voice that was missing was his mother's, whose prayers had dropped out early to be replaced by her steady, even breathing.

"I think Mom's asleep," Scott whispered to Abby after ending their prayer with an *Amen*.

"Poor thing," Abby commiserated. "I'm sure she couldn't have gotten any sleep last night, and once they locked her in here, she was probably too worried about you to rest."

"And carrying all our weight on her back probably didn't help any. I'm not completely convinced we didn't hurt her, no matter what she says."

"She might be stronger than you think," Abby said softly.

Scott was about to protest when he realized Abby was right. A weaker woman would have been tucked into the fetal position sobbing after all she'd been through. But remarkably, his mom had demonstrated a positive attitude, and had played a vital role in boosting Tracie out of the cave. "That must be where I get it from," he admitted in a teasing voice.

Abby jabbed him with her elbow, and he chuckled. He recognized how odd it was that he should be laughing in the face of danger, but after the relief of boosting Tracie through the fissure, and especially after their time of prayer, Scott felt a heightened level of security in God's love. He hadn't ever tested God's protection so much before, but after the miraculous way God had helped them so far, he felt God's love in a more intimate way than he had before, even though he prayed daily in his job as a Christian counselor.

"For when I'm weak, then I'm strong," Abby murmured beside him.

"What's that?"

"Oh, just that I didn't think we'd get Tracie out, that's all. But it wasn't about my strength or ability, it was about God's provision. I'm afraid I'd underestimated that before."

Scott had to smile. "You're right. God provides what we need—and He leads us when we don't know where we're going."

"He obviously led us here," Abby agreed. "I had no idea this was under here. I don't think anyone knew."

"Trevor must have." Scott didn't want to bring up the slain man's name again, but too much of the mystery before them still centered around Abby's ex.

"Do you think so?" Abby let out a long breath. "That's why he proposed to me, wasn't it? Too distract me, to keep me from seeing whatever was going on. I *did* hear voices that evening, didn't I?"

Scott pieced the story together in his head. "Trevor may have been standing on the island, communicating with someone who was going in or out of the cave."

"When he saw me, he realized I might see what was

going on, so he lifted me up and spun me around." Abby shook her head. "He set me down facing the opposite direction. How stupid of me! I didn't even think—"

"Didn't think what?" Scott wouldn't allow Abby to blame herself. "Didn't think about the fact that there might be something illegal going on under the island, and that the man proposing to you was only doing so to cover for them? Abby, you couldn't have known. I can still hardly believe this is down here. Let go of your guilt."

Abby fumed beside him. "Still," she huffed, "I could just kick myself for letting him fool me so easily."

"You know what I can't stand?" One nagging thought had been bothering him ever since he'd realized the family land was in danger. "I let my family down."

"No, you didn't," Abby protested. "You found your mother."

But the heaviness that weighed upon him wasn't shaken by her uplifting words. "Not my mother. The land. The Frasier family legacy. Even if Tracie gets help, even if Sal and his guys are caught, it doesn't matter. The Frasier family ends with me. I don't have an heir to leave it to. Sal and his guys spotted a great opportunity and took unfair advantage of the situation, true, but I walked right into their trap. What if Mom and I died in a real accident, without Captain Sal's intervention? Some developer would just sweep in and buy the land. I've failed them."

"We'll get out of this," Abby said softly.

"No, Abby, you were right." Scott's regret poured from him. "I've tried to do it all myself, tried to carry everyone else's load alone. But you know what? I'm just one man. I'm not invincible. If I pile everything on my own shoulders, when I fall, it all comes crashing down. I've isolated myself for far too long, and now my self-sufficient pride will be the downfall of my whole family." He shook his head remorsefully. "If I get out of this, I'm going to change some things."

"*When* we get out of this, what would you change?"

"I always wanted a family," Scott mused. "What about you, Abby?"

"Well, yes, of course." She sounded hesitant. "I always thought I would. I guess I just never met the right guy."

Her words struck Scott with force. So she didn't think of him as being the right guy? He tried to think of a way to ask her to explain what she meant, but before he could straighten out his thoughts, a harsh voice shouted, "Up and at 'em. We're going on a little trip."

FOURTEEN

Abby struggled to her feet, fear pounding through her.

"Come on, move it!" the harsh voices shouted. Light flashed against the barrels of the guns the men waved.

Trying to focus on following orders, Abby noticed Marilyn looked particularly disoriented by being so rudely awakened, and Abby kept close to her back, mindful they didn't want their captors to see the way the ropes hung askew from her wrists. At the same time, she looked around, taking in the changes the thugs had made in the cavern since they'd been brought in.

The computers, boxes and crates had all disappeared, leaving gaping black space the length of the cave. Likewise, the yacht was gone. Only the *Helene* remained.

They hurried obediently down the pier and were greeted by an outraged shout from Captain Sal. "Where's the other woman?"

"There were only three in the cave, sir," a gunman answered.

"We only put three in, as I recall," another muttered.

"This woman was already in there." Captain Sal pointed at Marilyn. "One of the other women is missing—the Coast Guard girl." He pointed his gun at a couple of the men.

"You two, go back and look for her. The rest of you, hurry up. If she's missing, we have even less time to waste!"

The thugs hurried them across a wide plank that led onto the *Helene*. Abby wished she knew what their plans were, but she figured it was in her best interest to get out of the cave, and since the boat was most likely headed out to sea, it appeared to be her best bet for the moment. Besides, the men still had their guns trained on them. It wasn't as though she was likely to easily escape, under the circumstances.

They were herded into the *Helene*'s small cabin and left alone. Abby could hear shouting on the outside. She figured Captain Sal was still trying to find Tracie.

Abby realized Marilyn had never told them what had happened with her while they'd been separated. She wondered what other helpful tidbits the woman might have picked up. "How many men are there? Do you have any idea?"

"There must be close to a dozen, that I've seen," Marilyn explained. "And they appear to be busy, too. I don't know what it's all about, but I'd guess it's some sort of smuggling ring."

The shouting outside grew louder.

"She's not?" Captain Sal sounded furious.

Another voice broke in. "Take them out! And hurry! If we're compromised—" The man continued speaking, but Abby could no longer make out what he was saying. The engine started up.

"We're headed out to sea," Marilyn observed.

Abby had figured as much. "What do we do?"

"I can't tell for sure how many men are on the boat—" Scott sat facing the cabin door, with the best vantage point from which to see the deck "—but I think it's just us and Sal."

"We can take him!" Marilyn declared optimistically.

"Mother, he's got a gun. It's too dangerous."

"But if he plans on using it on us anyway—"

"We need to get moving," Abby insisted, feeling a growing sense of fear and urgency. "We've got to act while we still can."

"Hold on." Scott strained his head to one side. "I can't see Captain Sal anymore."

"Can you see anyone else?" Marilyn asked.

"I don't see any movement out there."

"Let's get going!" Abby pleaded, starting to rise. She caught a whiff of a smell she didn't like. "Do you smell gasoline? And smoke?"

"I smell a gas fire," Marilyn fairly screamed. "If that hits the gas tank, we'll blow." She ripped her arms free of her bounds.

Abby and Scott followed suit, tugging off their slip-knots, rushing to the door of the cabin, and throwing their weight against it. It didn't budge. Scott pressed his face to the window and nudged aside the small curtain. "He's got a chair in front of it."

"Windows?" Marilyn asked.

Abby looked at the slender glass slits that served as windows for the small cabin. There was no way any of them would fit through.

But Scott had already leaped into action. He wrenched at the tabletop, which proved to be bolted to the floor. Abby scrambled underneath and tried to wiggle the bolts with her fingers.

"Rusted." She shook her head. "It won't budge." She crawled out from under the table in time to see Marilyn pulling open cupboards.

"Stand back!" Marilyn screamed, swinging an aluminum water pitcher at the windowpane in the door. It shattered, and she used the pitcher to scrape at the sides, hastily removing most of the glass shards.

Scott was right behind her. He reached through the opening, shoved the chair out of the way, and rammed the door open. The three of them spilled out onto the deck.

Smoke filled the air, and quickly filled their lungs. The boat was barreling into the open sea with no one at the wheel.

"We've got to jump overboard!" Scott shouted. He wrenched off the top of his wetsuit and shoved it over his mother's head.

Abby quickly realized what he was doing. The two of them would last longer wearing their wet suits—his mother had no such protection against the cold water. Abby grabbed the lone round life preserver that hung by the cabin door. She thrust it into Marilyn's hands just as Scott screamed, "Hurry! Jump!"

He pulled his mother over the edge of the boat in his arms. Abby scrambled up after them, looking to see where they'd landed so she wouldn't jump on top of them. She took a deep breath of the smoke-filled air.

As she leaped free of the boat, she heard the mighty explosion, and felt the searing heat of the flames. Then everything went dark.

Scott began swimming away from the *Helene* the moment he hit the water. Though he knew how frigid the waters of Lake Superior would feel, the shock of the cold water hitting his body still stunned him, even with the added insulation of his hydroskin pants. The way his mother shrieked and clung to him, he knew the icy waters had shocked her as well.

He felt the wave of heat as the *Helene* blew, and immediately looked back for some sign of Abby. She'd been right behind him, but he'd never heard her hit the water. He paddled with his right arm as he held his mother tight to him with his left and angled his body back until he could see the flaming wreckage of the *Helene.* For a moment, there was only white smoke and dark water and bright orange flames. Then he spotted Abby's still form, floating facedown far too close to the flaming wreckage.

His mother must have seen her as well. "Help Abby," she insisted through chattering teeth. She shoved the life preserver toward him.

Scott shoved it back. "Keep it. Try to get as much of your body as possible up out of the water. I can swim faster without." Before his mother could protest, he let go of her and kicked away toward Abby. The chill of the water against the bare skin of his arms was almost more than he could stand, but he forced himself to move forward as quickly as he could. Abby's life depended on it, and he could not, *would not* let Abby die.

The sound of the chopper's pounding blades beat against the inside of Abby's skull. She felt heavy and so very cold. There were arms around her, strong arms holding her tight, pulling her away from the cold, away from the tug of gravity that strained to drag her into the abyss.

"Abby, sweetheart, stay with me." The voice sounded familiar, like Scott's voice. She had to be dreaming. Had they only just wrecked their canoe off the shore of Rocky Island? Had everything else been a dream?

Then there were more hands on her, tugging her, moving her; and voices talking, asking questions, seeking a response. She didn't know the answers, didn't know how to answer, didn't know anything but the deep, bone-numbing cold, and the darkness that pulled her back.

The lights were too bright. When Abby tried to open her eyes, the beams of light hit her like spears, and she pinched her eyes shut again. The darkness called to her, wrapping its arms around her. She remembered the darkness, flew to it like an old friend, but it was different now. It wasn't a cold darkness. It was warm.

She became aware of her surroundings slowly. She was in the hospital in Duluth. They'd brought her there by helicopter—by Coast Guard helicopter. The nurses had to explain the story to her several times before it finally registered. Abby tried to ask them about Scott, but no one knew anything about him.

The news sank in slowly. It was over. Marilyn had been rescued. Scott didn't need her anymore. She wondered if she'd ever see him again. But why would she? She'd only ever be the girl whose ex-fiancé had shot his stepdad. At best, she was a girl he'd known years ago at school. They had nothing to bind them together now—nothing but Devil's Island. And she was never going to go back there.

Her family arrived a few hours later, her mother and father and younger sister, all of them appalled to hear what had happened, and confused when Abby tried to explain the details. She wondered if she was having trouble keeping the story straight, or if there were too many details she hadn't sorted through yet.

Tracie visited that evening. "You gave us all quite a

scare," she said by way of greeting as she handed over the purse Abby had left on the Coast Guard boat.

Abby smiled broadly at the sight of Tracie's familiar face, and was glad she'd finally shooed her family off to get her some food. At least she and Tracie could talk alone.

"You must have reached help in time." Abby raised her hospital bed so she could sit up straight.

"Yes. I ran to the keeper's quarters and we brought out the copters. When we got around to the north side of the island, we spotted a yacht heading north toward Canada. One helicopter went after them, and the helicopter I was in pulled you out of the water." Tracie sat in the visitor's chair beside Abby's hospital bed.

"The yacht," Abby said, remembering. "Did you catch it?"

"Of course. We caught a bunch of bad guys and an amazing haul of diamonds. The initial inspection says they're real, but I've got a sneaking suspicion they're the same kind as these clever fakes the FBI recently sent us a report on. They're almost impossible to spot, but at the same time, they're exactly the same."

"What about Captain Sal? Did he get away?"

"That's the best news of all. We picked him up paddling an inflatable life raft back toward the island. We've questioned him extensively. His story agrees with what Tim told you. Trevor had been working for these guys for years."

"I was afraid of that." Abby pinched her eyes shut. "So why did they kill him?"

"Apparently somebody was upset with Trevor for killing Mitch and taking his ring and phone. We're assuming that somebody was Captain Sal himself, but of course he hasn't admitted to that part."

Abby figured that only made sense. Then she heard the sound of someone clearing their throat in her doorway.

Tracie looked over and smiled. "Oh, that's right. And there's someone here to see you."

"Scott?" Abby gasped without thinking.

"Sorry, no." Tim Price stepped into the room. He wore a hospital robe, and though his eyes were rimmed with tired circles, he looked far more lucid than he'd been at The Brick.

"Oh, Tim." Abby apologized and smiled a genuinely warm smile. "I'm glad to see you here. Are you—"

"He turned himself in and is cooperating with the investigation," Tracie explained.

"I'm also getting detoxified." Tim gestured to his hospital-issued clothes. "Getting my act together." He looked at Tracie solemnly. "They killed my brother. I don't want to end up the same way. I have to get clean so I can bring his killers to justice."

"Oh, Tim." Abby's throat swelled. She'd felt awful for having turned her back on him all those years, especially once she'd seen what had become of him. "I'm so glad you're doing better. I should have looked you up sooner."

Tim nodded. "I missed you." His voice sounded hoarse. "I missed going to church with you."

Abby opened her mouth to offer him to come to church with her that Sunday, but then she stopped. After everything she'd experienced in Bayfield, she wasn't sure how safe she felt there. She'd been thinking of relocating—soon.

Fortunately, Tracie stepped in. "You'll be in treatment in Superior for the next twenty-eight days, but if you like, I'll come up and go to church with you."

"Would you? Thanks. I guess I could always go by

myself, too." He pushed back his tousled hair. "I need to apologize to you, Abby."

"To me? What for?"

"I'm the reason you and Trevor got engaged all those years ago."

Abby's eyebrows shot up at his statement.

"You were the nicest person I knew," Tim explained. "I hated it when I heard Trevor was planning to break up with you. So, one day I was helping him go through some of the jewelry that had come in, and I came across a ring that was just your size, and I told him to carry it with him, to propose to you. I told him you were the best thing that ever happened to him. He wasn't real excited about the idea, but he put it in his pocket. He told me later you came up on him just as he was watching a shipment head out. He didn't want you to see, so he proposed to distract you." Tim looked sheepish. "I know neither of you were really happy together. I felt awful once I realized what I'd done."

"It's okay, Tim." Abby reached for his hand and gave it a squeeze. "I should have stayed friends with you even after I broke up with your brother. Our friendship should never have depended on anything else."

"We can be friends now, though, can't we?" Tim asked.

"Of course," Abby assured him. She thought for a moment. "Can I ask you something—about the diamond smugglers?"

"Sure. What?"

"You said they wanted a piece of land, that Mitch was supposed to help them get it, but that they'd figured out a way that they didn't need him anymore. I guess I never really understood how that could be."

Tim shrugged and leaned on the rail of her hospital bed. "The way I understand it, Scott's name was never on the

property. It all went to his mother, and would have gone
straight to him if she would have died first. But Mitch got
Marilyn to put the land in their name jointly. Then Sal and
his guys had Mitch write his own will, leaving all the land
to them if anything happened to him. They'd been business
partners from way back."

"And that would work? Even though Mitch was killed
while Scott and Marilyn were still alive?"

"They figured they had an airtight case, but Sal still
wasn't too happy about Trevor getting rid of Mitch so
soon. I figure that's why he—" Tim's voice gave out and
he looked down.

Abby still had hold of his hand and gave it a squeeze.
"I'm sorry, Tim."

"I am, too." Tim nodded. "I'm sorry all this had to
happen to you and Marilyn and Scott."

At the mention of Scott's name, Abby felt a bittersweet
pain in her heart. She tried to remind herself that Scott had
never been a part of her life, so she had no business missing
him now. She had no right to feel heartbroken at the
thought of him. But knowing that didn't change the way
she felt. "It's okay. God was watching over us."

"You're right," Tim agreed, hope bringing a warm glow
to his face. "I think God put you on that boat with Marilyn
and Scott so you could save their lives."

Abby blushed. "I—I don't know that I really *saved* them."

"I believe you did," Tracie noted. "And Scott saved your
life, too, you know. He pulled you out of the water and
insisted we fly you straight here. He'd probably be here right
now if he didn't feel his proper place is with his mother."

Abby shook her head. "Scott and I aren't really a
couple," she rushed to explain. "We hardly knew each

other before this weekend. We probably won't see each other anymore after this."

But Tracie just grinned that much more broadly. "That's not what he told me."

Abby was alone again the next morning as she packed her things in preparation for her dismissal from the hospital. She didn't have much, just some flowers and candy her folks had brought, along with a change of clothes. Her parents and sister would be returning from their hotel within the hour to drive her home. With a sigh, she pulled her cell phone from her purse and looked at the screen.

She had plenty of signal and power remaining. It seemed strange that so much could happen within the time frame of a single cell phone charge. She absently scrolled down through her saved numbers, stopping when she came to Scott's.

Should she call him? She wanted to. She missed him already, and wished they could talk, if only to sort out the events of the weekend and find some closure from it all.

Abby flipped her phone shut and placed it back in her purse. She'd call Scott, but not right now. Later, when she had more time to talk.

A rap at the door caught her attention, and she looked up, expecting to see one of the nurses, or possibly her folks. Instead, Scott's strong frame filled the doorway, an uncertain smile on his lips.

"Scott." Her voice sounded breathless to her own ears, and she wanted to run to him, to throw herself into his arms, but instead she held back. After all, she hadn't heard from him in over a day. He apparently hadn't been too eager to see her.

"I'm sorry I couldn't get here sooner." He stepped into the room. "I had to talk to the authorities, and take care of our cars, and explain to my mother about Mitch."

"Uh-huh." Abby nodded dumbly. She'd almost forgotten about crashing her car, with everything else that had been happening.

Scott continued. "And you wouldn't believe how many jewelry stores I had to visit to find what I was looking for."

Abby watched him cross the room toward her. She couldn't fathom what jewelry stores had to do with anything. After all the trouble the diamonds had caused, she didn't care to ever see another one. "How many?" she asked, watching with curiosity as a smile toyed across his lips.

"Seven," he announced, pulling a small box from his pocket. "Practically every jewelry store in the Duluth-Superior metro area, I believe."

Though she still wasn't sure what he was getting at, Abby couldn't keep the corners of her mouth from turning up in response to his smile. "What were you looking for?" she prompted him.

"A sapphire ring," he explained. "But not just any sapphire. It had to have tiny flecks of gold dancing in the field of blue. And the blue had to be just the right color." Scott opened the jewelry box and held it up to her. His smile broadened. "Good. I got it right."

Abby's mouth fell open. "Just the right color?" she repeated dumbly.

"To match your eyes," Scott explained. "That *is* what you said you wanted, isn't it?"

Nodding eagerly, Abby sniffed back the sudden tears that threatened to overwhelm her. "But I thought—" she started.

"Thought what?" he asked. "Thought I wanted to spend the rest of my life alone? Maybe I used to think that, but not anymore. When I saw you floating facedown in the water, I felt fear like I've never felt before. Do you recall what I said yesterday, about how I was reluctant to care too much for someone, because the people I cared about almost always died?"

"Yes." Abby remembered him telling her about his father's and grandparents' deaths.

"I've pushed away everyone but God, trying to insulate myself from caring too much for other people, trying to keep that kind of hurt from ever reaching me again. I even pushed away my mother—I'm afraid that may have contributed to her turning to Mitch for emotional support." He shook his head regretfully. "I tried to push you away, too, but that didn't change anything, because I still felt as though I'd had my heart ripped from my chest when I saw you floating there."

Abby squeezed her eyes shut, somehow knowing how he felt, feeling the same pain at the thought of never seeing him again.

"I need you in my life, Abby. Pushing you away only makes it hurt worse, not less." Scott got down on one knee. "Abby, I know you said you hadn't met the right man yet, but I believe I've met the woman for me. You're the one. I let you slip through my fingers nine years ago. I won't make the same mistake again. Please, Abby, would you reconsider?"

Abby's eyes filled with tears. "Oh, Scott." She cupped his face with one hand. "I didn't mean you weren't the man for me. I was trying to say I hadn't met the right man at the right time, but then we got interrupted. I never meant to make you think I didn't love you."

A relieved smile broke over Scott's face. "So you love me then? You'd consider marrying me?"

His words seemed almost too good for Abby to believe. "But how would that work? You live in the Twin Cities, and I live in Bayfield."

"You know, after all she's been through, I think I need to move closer to my mother."

Abby looked at him quizzically.

"But not too close," Scott noted. "I was thinking of maybe moving to Bayfield."

"Ooh, that's awfully remote," Abby chided him. "And I don't really feel safe there after everything that happened. I was thinking of moving farther south myself."

"Really?" Scott smiled. "Perhaps we could settle on someplace close together."

"Perhaps." Abby looked back down at the ring in his hands. The color of the stone was remarkably similar to her eye color. Scott had clearly been paying very close attention.

"Well, then, I guess there's only one question left." Scott pulled the ring from the box. "Abby Caldwell, will you marry me?"

"I'd love to."

Scott stood and slid the ring onto her finger. Then he wrapped his arms around her and finally gave her the kiss she'd been longing for.

* * * * *

Dear Reader,

I've always loved survival stories. So when I moved to the remote village of Bayfield, Wisconsin, my imagination was quickly captured by the Apostle Islands, whose isolated wilderness seemed almost uninhabitable. After researching the islands, I started to write a story about a girl who was marooned on Devil's Island and left to die. Long before I finished my story, life intervened, and my half-finished manuscript was pushed aside. But I never stopped wondering how the story would end.

It has been a blessing to finally find the happy ending I always wanted the story to have. Scott and Abby have found their happy ending, but Devil's Island holds many secrets, and more stories to come. Visit my Web site at www.rachellemccalla.com for more information about upcoming books!

May all God's blessings go with you!

Rachelle McCalla

QUESTIONS FOR DISCUSSION

1. Abby buried the ring on Devil's Island as a way of moving beyond a painful era in her life. What painful experiences have you had to move past? What helped you heal?

2. Abby and Scott both liked each other during college, but neither knew the other felt the same. How might their relationship have been different if they'd gotten together sooner? How might they be better off for the delay? Have you ever missed out on a blessing by not sharing how you truly felt?

3. Marilyn allowed Mitch to influence her in making decisions that would ultimately hurt her. Is there anyone in your life who has such a strong influence over you? Has this influence been helpful or hurtful? How can you protect yourself from harm?

4. When Scott and Abby were marooned on Devil's Island, their initial response was denial, then helplessness. However, with God's help, they quickly strategized their escape. Have you ever felt stuck or left behind? How did you move past that?

5. Abby and Scott quickly realized they had to trust one another in order to escape Devil's Island. When have you had to make a "leap of trust" in order to achieve a common goal? How did it turn out for you? Have

you ever felt as though you were making that same leap in trusting God? How did that turn out?

6. Scott worked hard to protect his mother, Marilyn, from difficult situations, but he eventually learned she was stronger than he thought. Is there anyone in your life you've sheltered? Who has sheltered you? Has this been helpful or problematic?

7. Abby observed that Trevor seemed driven to torture her. Have you ever known anyone who has acted this way? How did you respond to their behavior? Why do you think they acted that way?

8. When Scott discovered Captain Sal and Mitch had been plotting for a long time to take the Frasier family land, Scott felt foolish for not recognizing what was happening. Abby told Scott he'd had no reason to suspect what was going on. Do you ever feel guilty about things you couldn't realistically have prevented? How do you cope with your feelings of guilt? What have you learned from that experience?

9. Mitch may have been a villain at first, but he soon became a victim of the devious plot he was involved in. When people welcome evil deeds into their lives, the evil often backfires and can ultimately consume them. Have you experienced anything like this in your life? In the lives of people you know? How did you respond?

10. In Abby's desire to help Scott find his mother, Abby was willing to visit a frightening place (The Brick) and

to revisit a person from her past (Tim). Have you ever gone somewhere frightening or faced a person from your past in order to help a friend? How did it turn out?

11. Do you think it was foolish of Abby to go to The Brick alone? How could she have protected herself from danger?

12. As Scott's love for Abby grew, he tried to keep her from helping in order to shield her from harm, even though he was willing to take risks himself. How did Abby feel about Scott's decision? What arrangement did they reach? How do you protect those you love?

13. Scott had experienced many losses and was frightened about getting close to Abby for fear he would be hurt again. How did he overcome his fear? How have you dealt with loss in your life? What strategies have helped you love again?

14. The pirate's cave was well hidden under Devil's Island, and the authorities had never realized it was there. Sometimes people in our lives hide things that turn out to be huge once discovered, and we wonder how we missed seeing their secret. What secrets have people hidden from you? What secrets are you hiding? Is it time to uncover your secret? See Psalm 32:3–5 for more insights on this topic.

15. Though Scott and Abby both felt attracted to each other years before, they were reunited only a short time before becoming engaged. Do you think they

should have taken their relationship more slowly? What aspects of their relationship do you think will help make their marriage successful? What might work against them? Do you believe they will live happily ever after?

Read on for a sneak preview of
KATIE'S REDEMPTION
by Patricia Davids,
the first book in the heartwarming new
BRIDES OF AMISH COUNTRY *series*
available in March 2010
from Steeple Hill Love Inspired.

When a pregnant formerly Amish woman returns
to her brother's house, seeking forgiveness
and a place to give birth to her child,
what she finds there isn't what she expected.

*P*lease, God, don't let them send me away.

To give her child a home Katie Lantz would endure the angry tirade she expected from her brother. Through it all Malachi wouldn't be able to hide the gloating in his voice.

An unexpected tightening across her stomach made Katie suck in a quick breath. She'd been up since dawn, riding for hours on the jolting bus.

Her stomach tightened again. The pain deepened. Something wasn't right. This was more than fatigue. It was labor.

Breathing hard, she peered through the blowing snow. It wasn't much farther to her brother's farm. Closing her eyes, she gathered her strength.

One foot in front of the other. The only way to finish a journey is to start it.

She sagged with relief when her hand closed over the railing. She was home.

Home. The word echoed inside her mind, bringing with it unhappy memories that pushed aside her relief. Raising her fist, she knocked at the front door. Then she bowed her head and closed her eyes, grasping the collar of her coat to keep the chill at bay.

When the door finally opened, she looked up to meet her brother's gaze.

Katie sucked in a breath and then took a half step back. A tall, broad-shouldered Amish man stood in front of her with a kerosene lamp in his hand and a faintly puzzled expression on his handsome face.

It wasn't Malachi.

To read more of Katie's story,
pick up KATIE'S REDEMPTION
by Patricia Davids, available March 2010.

Love Inspired®

HEARTWARMING INSPIRATIONAL ROMANCE

Love Inspired®

Easter Promises
Lois Richer
Allie Pleiter

Two heartwarming Easter stories that celebrate the renewal of love, life and faith.

2 NEW STORIES IN 1 BOOK

From two bestselling authors comes this volume containing two heartwarming Easter stories that celebrate the renewal of love, life and faith.

Easter Promises
by
Lois Richer and Allie Pleiter

Available March wherever books are sold.

LARGER-PRINT BOOKS!

GET 2 FREE
LARGER-PRINT NOVELS
PLUS 2 FREE
MYSTERY GIFTS

Love Inspired®
SUSPENSE
RIVETING INSPIRATIONAL ROMANCE

Larger-print novels are now available...